T3-BNK-132

John J Wish

Phil Parrish

~~6848 60482 7505~~

THROWING STONES

STONES

By John Wasik & Phillip Parrish

~~PROPERTY OF~~
~~CALDWELL PUBLIC LIBRARY~~

FIC
WAS

Copyright ©2009, P&J Publishing

978-0-578-02860-6

All Rights Reserved. No part of this book may be reproduced or transmitted in any form or by any means, electronic or mechanical, including photocopying, recording, or by any information storage and retrieval system without written permission from the author, except for the inclusion of brief quotations in a review.

Printed in the United States of America.

The only thing necessary for the triumph of evil is for good men to do nothing.

—*Edmund Burke*

SPECIAL THANKS

We would like to acknowledge our friend and mentor Professor Robert James for all his patience and advice throughout the writing of this book. We would also like to thank artist Mary O. Skorpys for her work. And, to our wives, Jo and Pam, thanks for putting up with us.

THROWING STONES

TABLE OF CONTENTS

1 | MESSAGES FROM BAGHDAD

No one knows exactly when the conflict originated between East and West. Ever since Cain and Abel, true believers keep fighting. Some thousand-year-old feuds will never be resolved. An eye taken from one man was worth taking the eye from another. Disputes over oil, political control and religious ideology have replaced land, water and gold. Whereas the West has progressed to guided missiles, spy satellites and cluster bombs, there are fighters who still symbolically resort to throwing stones.

Thinking back, I deliberated what motivated the killers who hurled those jet planes into the World Trade Center. In the last millennium, the concept of protecting ourselves from terrorists' attacks was not the all-consuming commodity. Today, we are more vigilant. We sacrifice civil liberties in the name of uniting against an invisible enemy, whose pent-up anger is exploding throughout the world. Many have a sense of duty to defend our democratic culture, yet feel powerless to change our collective fate. I do not recall who said, "All things are as they should be, else they would be otherwise." We must find a way to turn off the spigot of hate that is pouring over the world. Nonetheless, we pay scant attention to others' ideology until their beliefs threaten our way of life.

I became personally involved when my nephew Jusef's name turned up in a routine investigation that uncovered a terrorist cell.

As layers of secrecy peeled away like an onion, each skin of evidence indicated my nephew was involved in a plot to attack the United States. From my point of view, in places where the sands of time stood still, Western intrusions have awakened an anger in these isolated people who sent a message on 9/11.

Jusef was not born a terrorist. He embraced Western culture until a short time ago. Somehow, he fell into step with thousands of other young men attracted to the beat of rebellion. He marched into war against the West under the mullah's cadence. A colleague asked what made me an expert on terrorism. My reply came quickly: Murder evokes fear. Once one evokes fear in his enemy—he has won—even if only to claim a moral victory. I caution colleagues to beware of arbitrarily labeling a person a terrorist; for in reality, he might be trying to right a wrong. Others have often said that one man's terrorist is another man's freedom fighter. When governments declare war, their generals move soldiers like pieces in a deadly game of chess, with an opening gambit, a middle-game attack and a strategy for victory. For those fighting to overcome injustice, each day is a life and death struggle until they achieve their purpose. From the beginning, I have tried to keep this subtle distinction in mind.

History keeps records of leaders and militant organizations, leaving the individual warriors anonymous. Many Middle Eastern conflicts have been forgotten, along with thousands of loyal soldiers. Warring factions passed down feuds and traditions to the next generation. While some fled foreign lands to escape these internal conflicts, others remained behind to carry on the battle and fend for themselves. Unwritten rules replaced their steady tribal rudder, setting a course and propelling them into direct conflict with the government. Eventually, tribal members developed a mindset of resistance to foreign influence. Over time, a holy war has emerged, ignited from a spark, sending flames far beyond the Middle East.

This cunning enemy, Tarik Lazar, code-named *the Lizard* was committed to fight for values he held sacred. I have no doubt *the Lizard* was prepared to die or sacrifice countless others to defend his beliefs and way of life. Without question, this master terrorist, who I pursued from my home in Hamburg, Germany to the United States, changed my life forever.

The jingle of a brass bell alerted the lone man working late when someone entered Sam's Deli. He did not recognize the black-haired customer sporting a mustache and wearing a black leather jacket. A turned up seaman's collar partially concealed the shopper's face. The solitary proprietor watched the figure scurry like a silent rat to the furthest aisle and disappear behind a display of dust-covered cereal boxes. The owner nervously glanced at one of four fisheye mirrors that hung in each corner. He reached under the counter to reassure himself his weapon was available. Again, the brass bell announced two more arrivals. Both men wore black three-quarter-length jackets. A hidden lens captured each individual's middle-eastern features. The man with a shaved head appeared to be in his mid-twenties, his right hand concealed in his coat pocket as he stood near the entrance.

Instantly recognizing the older one approaching him from a previous visit to his store, the man behind the counter shouted, "I told you never to come back into my store."

The unwelcome visitor continued to walk toward him. With his arms extended and hands open, the lone clerk's heart began to pound. He completely forgot about the third man as his sweaty hand clutched the pistol under the counter.

"Get out, now!" he scolded while pointing with his freehand toward the exit. The concealed hand tightened around the butt of the Berretta pistol.

The older individual continued to advance cautiously. Dropping his hands, he stated, "How soon one forgets his people under the spell of American money. Our struggle will go on with or without you." He raised his voice and announced, "Everyone must pay."

The message caused the frightened man to pull out his pistol from under the counter. "You get nothing! Not one cent! Now get out, or I call police!" He aimed his pistol at the unwelcome visitor.

From the five o'clock portion, a cylindrical object came into view of the camera's eye. The muzzled barrel silently flashes twice, each time recoiling swiftly. The slugs punched into the side of the owner's head, causing flying human debris to paint the wall with a mural of death.

The older man turned to look back toward the sentry guarding the door. The bald individual nodded back, signaling that everything was okay to proceed. Turning toward the shooter, he spoke in a flat voice and ordered, "Finish him. Leave his gun. Take cash and cigarettes only."

The man with the turned up collar reappeared, and emptied three more bullets into the owner's head.

"Car 514, respond to a silent alarm at Sam's Deli, East 105 and Quincy."

"En route to 105 and Quincy," an officer radioed back to the dispatcher.

Several neighborhood people peered through the front windows. The moment the locals spotted the approaching patrol car, they scattered in opposite directions to disappear in alleyways and darkened corners. The first officer cautiously entered the delicatessen with pistol in hand. His partner followed. The distinct sound made by a round being chambered into his 12-gauge shotgun cleared the streets of curious bystanders.

The first police officer took five steps inside and froze. He assumed a defensive position while scanning the store left to right over the pistol's sight. He announced an initial warning, "Whoa! The place is covered in blood. I see at least three shell-casings on the floor." The second officer also assumed a defensive position and surveyed the crime scene. The lead officer approached the counter and glanced over. "There's a dead guy on the floor behind the counter."

"You sure he's dead?" the second officer inquired.

"Yeah, I'm sure. Half his head is missing. His gun is on the floor. Looks like he might have tried to defend himself," he informed his partner who had proceeded to check the other aisles.

"Register's empty. Looks like a robbery that went bad when he reached for his weapon." The second officer joined his partner to view the victim. He returned the 12-gauge intimidator to safety mode by putting the shell back in the magazine. "Someone had it in for this poor bastard; looks to me like he was executed. Maybe this was set up to look like a robbery," the second officer speculated.

The first officer holstered his pistol before activating his radio. "Get us a supervisor, homicide and SIU. We have a DOA at Sam's Deli at East 105."

The female dispatcher responded, "We're notifying them at 2300 hours."

Outside, a crowd of spectators re-gathered, some watching from a safe distance while others ventured to the store's window for a better view. Crime snooping mobile television crews raced to the scene to scoop the lead story for the following morning's news. The arrival of the first news van signaled the show had begun.

Exhausted and unable to sleep during the direct flight from Hamburg to Cleveland, I found myself constantly twisting from side to side attempting to find a comfortable dozing position. There was little to do but stare through heavy eyelids at the blue and white dots flickering across the blacked sky that filled the window to my right. On my left, my nephew slept seated upright without any worldly concerns. The sporadic rays of cabin light emitted an eerie shadow over Gabriel's facial contusions and abrasions. The thought of Jusef assaulting his cousin infuriated me. Families were supposed to help one another—not launch savage attacks. My frustration was depriving me of desperately needed rest for the mission that lies ahead.

The seatbelt light came on with the customary pinging noise prior to the captain announcing that the aircraft was beginning its final approach. Even without watching the flight attendants perform their final inspection, one could feel the sensation of descent. The stars disappeared as the plane dropped below the clouds. I turned toward Gabriel and gave him a gentle nudge.

Once we cleared Customs, my nephew and I rode the train from the airport to Tower City, then flagged a taxicab to our hotel—a ten-minute trip. We settled into room 714 at the downtown Holiday Inn. My nephew had no trouble completing his interrupted sleep. I, on the other hand, was not so fortunate.

The suite provided a panoramic view to the north. I witnessed the spectacle of nature's furry that blended the first rays of dawn with Canadian arctic winds that were marching rows of blue steel clouds southward over the city. With a little effort, one could easily imagine invisible hands stirring a caldron of restless dark-green waters that caused violent white-capped waves to assault the protecting rocks on the shoreline. Ice coated, leafless tree limbs trembled in the plaza below. Whistling winds marked the passing of autumn and approaching of winter. Glazed streetlamps and flagpoles swayed in a crosswind over an ice-crystal wonderland. The constant pinging sound against the flagpole marked the passing of time with each metal clash. One by one, streetlamps dimmed, giving way to a steel-gray morning.

Staying at Holiday Inns had become a habit. Whenever available, I book a middle-class travel's delight with full amenities to eliminate unpleasant surprises. This particular suite included a club chair with ottoman, a standing floor lamp, a desk with swivel chair, plus an additional telephone with wireless Internet. The sign in the bathroom proclaimed *a hospitality promise to make your stay satisfactory.*

"Uncle Thomas, what are you staring at?" Gabriel asked as he sat up in bed.

"Just thinking, what evil forces have done to us."

"What evil forces?" Gabriel questioned in a blurry-eyed moment of early morning confusion.

"Not just us. Our whole family and everyone we know."

My own words sent a chill through me. The possibility that we had traveled four thousand miles on a fruitless mission was unsettling. Before leaving Germany, I thought I knew exactly what needed to be accomplished: Rescue my nephew and prevent a catastrophe. Now, I was not sure Jusef was even in Cleveland. What if he was merely passing through, and had headed off in any number of directions. The nearly quiet streets below did not suggest any type of previously imagined catastrophe. Without hard data in hand, there was no way of legitimizing the otherwise scary thought that a pending terrorist attack in the United States might occur. I was annoyed with myself for not having contacted the State Department; or perhaps the local police. While not prone to second-guessing, especially myself, the underlying fact was that no one in his right mind would believe an unsubstantiated threat.

Each time we find ourselves in direct conflict with the private image we hold of ourselves, we run the risk of losing our self-confidence. I for one pride myself on being both logical and methodical. Americans, however, do not seem to understand themselves nor do they appear to appreciate such qualities. I had resolved myself to accepting that these foreigners do things differently. They seem to react, rather than take a proactive approach to things. As a result, I am not sure they will help me. If I go to the media with pictures of Jusef and his associates, the authorities here will no doubt become overly suspicious of my motives. They will ask me, "*Why didn't you go to the FBI?*"

That thought provoked another. For several moments, I contemplated my reason for not contacting the FBI. Perhaps I wanted to avoid the risk of becoming what they euphemistically refer to as: *a person of interest*—that individual is someone not to be trusted.

I turned toward Gabriel, still in bed, and asked, "I wonder who Jusef is masquerading as now?"

"Whose name was he using?" Gabriel inquired.

"Joseph Müeller."

"That is Uncle Joe's name!"

"Some people think they are smarter than the police. Jusef is one of them. That friend of his, Ali, is also using an alias. He entered Canada under the name Omar Al' Ebay with false papers."

"How do you know these things?" Gabriel asked with narrow, unfocused eyes.

"It is what I do. Now go back to sleep."

I glanced at the time, and then returned to the window. Staring at the endless motion of raging whitecaps took me back to '03; that last supper before our troubles began. The strong winds reminded me of Northern Germany, Sonja's dinner and the day I made my promise.

Sonja's cooking sent aromas of onions, garlic, peppers, and her secret spices throughout the apartment building. Her dinners were well worth the drive to Cologne. I followed the savory scent to the arched wooden door. My #1 rule as a bachelor is that one should never be late for a home-cooked meal.

My eighteen-year-old nephew answered my official knock on the heavy oak door. Framed in the doorway, Gabriel's stature indicated he had obviously sprouted up several millimeters since I saw him last. He was becoming a handsome young man with dark features and contrasting blue eyes.

Gabriel looked up to me from the beginning. As time went on, he admired my military and police service in Somalia and Afghanistan. Since my promotion to Chief Investigator in the Hamburg Police Department, he badgers me for details about my investigations.

I embraced Sonja on entering her kitchen. "How are you my dear?" Holding up a carton of ice cream, I said, "dessert." Inhaling the aromas from her famous veal paprikash, I asked, "Did you make spaetzel?"

She prodded me away, "Go sit in the living room. Two are a crowd in this one-butt kitchen."

Gabriel eagerly followed me into the front room, "What secret investigations are you working on?"

"There is always something important happening at work. Where is Assam?"

Neither one answered my question. *Perhaps they did not hear me.* I repeated, "Where is Assam?" Their silence aroused suspicion that something was wrong. I looked at Gabriel, who pretended to watch television. I observed Sonja's body quiver in the kitchen.

She struggled to say, "Baghdad," wiping tears from her eyes. Her voice returned to normal, "He is in Baghdad with Kristina and Jusef."

"Uncle Mohammed is dead!" Gabriel interposed.

"The colonel is dead—what happened?"

"Apparently he was killed in an explosion. We do not know the details. Thank God, Kristina and Jusef were not with him. The authorities suspect a car bomb, but they have provided no further information. Assam took the first available flight to Iraq to help them. I pray that he will be able to bring them back to Germany soon."

"Why did you not mention this to me before? Kristina is my sister, too." I questioned.

"She tried to call us the day Mohammed was killed, but they lost power. Fortunately, Jusef has a friend with a generator who was able to get an email through to us."

"How does Assam intend to bring them back?"

"I have no idea. Right now, he has a bigger problem," she added, "The German Consulate contacted me to verify Assam is my husband and why he is in Iraq. They asked questions about Kristina and where Jusef was born."

"Did they give any reason why are they checking up on them?"

"The Americans are holding his passport, so he went to the German Liaison for help."

"Why would the Americans hold his passport?"

"No one will tell them anything. Assam is being forced to stay in Baghdad. He thinks he is under surveillance."

"Fortunately, Kristina had enough sense to remain here until Jusef was born. Because they are both German citizens, Mohammed could have arranged for Kristina and Jusef to leave Baghdad before the war. Now you are telling me none of them can leave. This is an impossible situation! They are in the middle of a civil war."

Sonja continued, "I told him not to go, but you know how stubborn he is. You must do something."

"Nobody consulted me," I grumbled to myself, "but now you expect me to find a solution."

"You know people in the government; important people who can help."

"You are placing me in a particularly difficult position. Assam is not German. Our government considers him an Iraqi. He is literally without a country at the moment."

"Please, Thomas, you must do something. What about your connections in the government and your American friends," Sonja pleaded.

"My American contacts would be of little help in this matter."

I had hoped to avoid making a promise I could not keep. That would be unethical. As I mentally calculated several options, I selected the safest avenue.

"I will make a few unofficial inquiries."

"Maybe you can get them out in time for the family reunion."

"I will do my best."

Our family's annual picnic was a big event for Sonja, while for me the event was more about certain extended family members. Uncle Joe with his annoying accordion, for example, always attended the event. Then there was my outspoken cousin, William, who was vocal in his view that Germans during the war were merely brainwashed victims of the Nazis. My immutable relatives all played their parts.

Joe was not my favorite uncle, but I did admire some of his traits. He has managed to maintain his individuality along with an enduring mistrust for everyone and everything. His paranoia instilled in me never to put trust in anyone or anything a hundred percent—especially the government.

I embraced her and whispered, "You have my promise. Now would be a good time to change the subject."

"Thank you, Tommy. I love you."

"I love you, too, little sister."

I enjoyed spending time with family. During Sonja's dinner, I kept admiring my nephew. His deep blue eyes were a dominant family trait. Moreover, he appreciated the value of history, and was one of the few in the younger generation who actually listened. This alone sets him apart.

"What do the Americans want from my father?"

"My guess is they want his expertise to continue their fruitless search for nuclear weapons."

"If their effort is so fruitless, why continue?"

"Assam speaks Arabic, and he knows how to probe for evidence. I am certain the American government will spend a fortune in an attempt to validate their invasion and continued occupation. Once they admit their mistake, I am sure Assam will be allowed to return home."

From the beginning, I felt uncomfortable that this whole situation—no matter how well intended, was a bad idea. Assam was less than diplomatic at handling high-stress situations, which may have complicated his own situation by going to the diplomats. Maybe the worst idea was for Sonja and Assam not to call me when they first received a message from Baghdad.

There had been little progress in the five weeks since I made my promise to Sonja. Except for the 'chatter,' as the Americans referred to it, I learned of increased activity according to secured sources. Our Intelligence Section, MEK, had successfully identified suspected terrorist cells in Hamburg, Cologne, New York, Chicago, London and Madrid. The intelligence information indicated an unusually high amount of cell phone traffic along with an increased number of individuals passing through several major airports for the months of July and August. In turn, this triggered a security alert by the end of the month. Our SWAT Unit, SEK, as of September 1, was to assist the MEK by providing additional surveillance.

My sergeant, Karl Mayer had placed several messages in time order and priority on my desk. One message requested I call Gabriel. He was out of school when I reached him.

"This is your Uncle Thomas. Did you call?"

"Yes, I received a message from Baghdad," Gabriel announced.

"Telephone or email?"

"Cousin Jusef sent me an email, Uncle. He will arrive in three days. How did you get them out?" Gabriel yelled.

"No need to shout. I am not deaf, yet. I made a few inquiries with contacts in Baghdad. The process still took a month longer than I had hoped." I continued sifting through the pile of papers, while speaking. "Question: I have a message from our Consulate. Does the name Ali mean anything to you?"

"Yes. Jusef has an orphan friend named Ali. His parents were killed in a bombing several months ago. He has been living with Jusef and Aunt Kristina ever since."

"I am reading as I speak, so be patient. The message from our Consul says Kristina will be staying in Iraq with your father until they can both come home."

"I was hoping to see father sooner, but this is still good news. May I go with you to the airport to pick up Jusef and Ali?" Gabriel asked.

"No. This will be less difficult if I go alone. However, I need a small favor. Could you possibly make contact with either Assam or Kristina via email?"

"I do not know. Cousin Jusef was using the computer at the mosque because they have a generator. Most of Baghdad has no reliable power," Gabriel informed me.

"If you reach them, tell Assam I will meet them at the airport. Let your mother know I will see her in two days, once I pick up Jusef."

"Sure. See you soon," Gabriel replied.

"And, could you also forward that email to me?"

Upon replacing the receiver, I summoned Sergeant Karl Mayer. I informed him of the incoming email that originated from Baghdad. Knowing the mosque had a computer operated by a generator was an interesting piece of information. Rocking back in my chair, I reflected on how such equipment might be used, and informed Karl to check out all communications to and from the mosque.

Within the hour, Karl handed me several communications that had been sent across the World Wide Web. One appeared different and piqued my interest. The message read:

To: Acme, Inc., Region 5 Office

From: Main Office

Two new apprentices have been recruited. They show much promise. They will attend our training classes before coming to assist you with your current project. Training center will update you on course completion and expected arrival at your location.

Moments later, the Project Manager responded:

To: Main Office

From: Project Manager

Message understood.

I asked Karl, "Who is this individual? Where is he? And what is he up to?"

Without further exchange, Karl established this as a priority. All the responding emails were identified by region numbers, except for this one. I strongly suspected this individual held an important position in the organization.

2 | SAFE AND SECURE

Tᴀʀɪᴋ Lᴀᴢᴀʀ sᴜᴍᴍᴏɴᴇᴅ Yᴀssᴀʀ ᴛᴏ ᴛʜᴇ ʙᴀᴄᴋʀᴏᴏᴍ ᴏꜰꜰɪᴄᴇ ᴡɪᴛʜ 1960-style wood paneling. There were no windows to the outside world, which ensured privacy. The Project Manager held up the email, "We are getting two new recruits soon. Make the usual arrangements."

"Yes, Lizard."

Lazar shot back a disapproving look.

"Sorry, Mr. Lazar, I forgot myself, but no one in Cleveland knows you."

"We cannot afford mistakes. Get into the habit of never using that name—even in Arabic. You might slip up in public. Besides, you never know who is listening."

At 0930 hours the following day, I placed a telephone call to Jay, a long-time friend in Cleveland. Jay was old school and a fellow police officer who could be trusted to keep a secret. He possessed unwritten knowledge, and knew how to bend the law in order to get things done.

"Cleveland Police, S.I.U. This is Sergeant Andrewski. How may I help you?" the voice answered.

"Hello Jay? This is Thomas from Hamburg."

"What a surprise! What's the weather like in Hamburg?"

"I cannot say. I am calling you from downtown Cleveland."

"What the hell are you doing here? Why didn't you call and tell me you were coming?"

"I left on short notice. I am here on a personal matter."

"The *personal matter*, might this require official help?"

I took a deep breath before responding. My nature was neither to ask for favors, nor impose upon others—especially friends. Nothing wears down friendship faster than constantly asking for favors. Furthermore, I did not want to divulge too much over a landline.

"If my asking would not be too much trouble, I could use your assistance locating my nephew, Jusef. He is my sister Kristina's son."

"Okay. Refresh my memory," Jay requested.

"My younger sister, Kristina, moved to Baghdad with her husband and their son, Jusef. Her husband was killed, and Jusef returned to Germany, but has subsequently disappeared. We think he came to Cleveland."

"What makes you think he's here?"

"In the last email to Kristina, Jusef mentioned University Circle. I brought my other nephew along who believes Jusef is here. I want to make sure he does not find him first and take revenge. This way I can keep an eye on his activities, that is our secret. Naturally, Jusef might have already left the area, but chances are more likely he is still here. We will need your help in our search."

"Where are you now?" Jay inquired.

"—Holiday Inn Lakeside."

"I'll meet you in the hotel's restaurant in twenty minutes."

I returned the receiver and raised my voice, "Gabriel, wake up." After no response, I added, "Okay, I am going to breakfast."

Gabriel responded by moving to the edge of the bed and dropping one foot to the floor. A moment later, he sat upright. Like me, the mention of food effectively stimulated him.

I used a magnifying glass to inspect a navy-blue suit not hanging long enough in the closet. Systematically detecting and removing several specks of lint, I finished dressing with the inspection of my profile in the full-length mirror. My appearance revitalized my otherwise sleep-deprived deportment.

"Will I need to wear a sport coat?" Gabriel asked with a measure of protest.

"Wear the black wool sweater and a shirt. We will be taking breakfast with a friend of mine, so do one small favor. Refrain from asking too many questions. Jay is a very busy officer and we need his help."

We seated ourselves in the ground floor restaurant at one of the red vinyl-covered booths. From across the table, Gabriel watched me unfold a linen napkin to inspect each piece of silverware. As I began the process with my magnifying glass, Gabriel reached across the table and drummed his fingers on the tabletop. I ignored his distraction and began rubbing each utensil with a napkin.

A voice from behind said, "Those are only water spots from the dishwasher. The silverware is clean, honey." From over my shoulder, the smiling waitress placed two coffee mugs on the table.

"This is a bad habit of mine. Please do not be offended."

"A lot of people have nervous habits, honey."

"I am not nervous—just full of bad habits," I replied.

She speculated, "I thought maybe you were concerned about the recent shootings. The one last night has many people nervous. That was the second one in a week. So, what would you like? I recommend the buffet."

The suggestion appealed to Gabriel. I settled for the coffee she brought in a carafe. Observing about 20 business-type people in the restaurant, I was taken aback at my return to polishing the silverware, and changed the utensil inspections for coffee sipping. These distractions camouflaged my troubling thoughts, one of which was how to broach my suspicions to Jay.

I had been to the United States before, but now things seemed different. There was an unsettling sense this country had transformed itself. Perhaps not my place as a foreigner to pass judgments, I held the daunting observation that this otherwise fearless nation was conceivably morphing into a police state. Most Europeans viewed United States' foreign policy as diplomacy through intimidation. Americans seem to avoid asking themselves tough questions, like why is their government so despised abroad?

While sipping coffee, I recalled the last time I saw Jay two years earlier. We had driven to his weekend cottage on Seneca Lake in southern Ohio, which he affectionately referred to as his *hideout in the hills.* There I met Buck, a local handyman who was packing a pistol on his tool belt. To me, as foreign a place as Afghanistan appeared, I could not resist the idea that Americans have an obsession about carrying weapons.

"Wie gehts," Jay bellowed from across the restaurant, as he dodged chairs coming straight toward me. His brown and black striped suit made his six-foot-three stature look taller and thinner. Every brown hair was in place and combed straight back. The detective with distinguished gray sides smiled as he approached.

"I have been better, my friend."

Jay's smile disappeared. "I detected a sense of urgency when you called."

"I did not feel comfortable going into the details on the phone."

"I understand, my friend," Jay responded. He flagged the waitress, "I've been working all night. I need coffee, dear."

Upon my nephew's return from the buffet, Jay noted, "He looks like he's already bigger than you. Better slow him down a little."

"Mr. Andrewski, I am curious. My uncle mentioned that you are in charge of S.I.U. What does this mean?" Gabriel inquired.

"Call me Jay. S.I.U. stands for Scientific Investigations Unit. We gather and process evidence from crime scenes. Lab technicians perform a lot of technical work to follow up investigations. In short, we're the police department's forensic unit."

"Thank you for coming so soon," I replied. "Are you working on that shooting from last night?"

"That's pretty good detective work for someone who has only been in the country a few hours, but I can't discuss an open investigation. How can I help you, Thomas?"

"I do not want you to be alarmed, but I suspect that my nephew, Jusef, has become involved with a group of terrorists. Furthermore, I am convinced they are here. I do not know what they are planning, however, I am certain they are up to something. I called you for your assistance, and any suggestions you can offer."

"Have you reported your suspicions to anyone else?"

"I am working with MEK, our intelligence unit and BKA, our national police investigators. They have contacted Interpol, your CIA and presumably the FBI. They provided me with pictures of Jusef and his accomplice, Omar Al' Ebay. Both are traveling with false documents. They were traced on a flight from Europe to Montreal, Quebec. I suspect they are here in Cleveland."

"How can you be so sure?"

"My sister Kristina's last email from Jusef mentioned University Circle."

"When was this information sent?"

"One week ago. I checked back with our authorities and they informed me neither Jusef nor Ali returned to Europe. My office in Germany received a generic response from your FBI office in Europe that the matter is under investigation. Unfortunately, they provided no details."

"The Cleveland regional office has more than 200 FBI agents assigned here. Their headquarters is a couple blocks down the street. You might want to contact them. They are better equipped to handle international threats. However, just to back you up, keep me informed, and let me know what happens."

Jay handed me his business card with the contact's number on the back. He opened his cell phone and unsuccessfully tried placing a call. He turned and said, "My FBI contact isn't in. I'll drive you over there."

"Please, if the office is so close, we prefer to walk. The fresh air will do us good and Gabriel needs exercise after this breakfast."

With the wave of his hand, Jay signaled the waitress for the check. "My treat. The FBI building is three blocks on your left as you go east." Jay's cell phone rang. "That's my office; I have to take this call." For the next several moments, Jay silently nodded his head, and ended the call with, "Thanks."

"That was not good news," I stated, as I watched him return his phone.

"Okay, tell me how you know that?"

"Your body-language told me."

"Shit! None of the damn pellets and casings matched!" Jay appeared more upset now than when he was on the phone. "The MOs are exactly the same. The shooter has to be the same. I can taste it."

"Detective, how can you be so certain?" I returned.

Jay continued thinking aloud, "Each one was Arab. Each one was working alone. Both were shot execution style in an extremely brutal fashion. The killer or killers are out for revenge or want to send someone a message. I'd stake my experience that these are definitely not simple robberies." He suddenly stopped and made direct eye contact with me. "So, you think your nephew may be involved in these shootings?"

"Why would you say that?"

Jay smiled, "I also read body language."

Gabriel and I left the hotel at the corner of Cardinal Joseph Mindszenty and Lakeside Avenue. The October air was brisk, so we walked quickly to our destination. We completed the 10-minute walk in 5.

Gabriel complimented, "Uncle Thomas, you are lucky to have such a good friend."

"True, we have known each other since the early nineties. I met him on one of my visits through the International Police Association."

The Lake Erie wind whipped against our faces as we scurried for three blocks toward the FBI Building. We approached the entrance to the concrete fortress ringed with nine-foot high walls. *Federal Bureau of Investigation* identified this structure as the Cleveland branch office. Upturned collars shielded our heads and features from the protective eyes attached to the building.

We walked through the open gates of the electrified metal barrier that surrounded the compound. Gabriel wanted to use the elevator alongside the stairs, but I insisted we walk the dozen or so stairs to the main lobby. The concrete steps split around the FBI Seal and reconnected at the landing.

The building reminded me of embassies overseas. Fortifications are a major concern for all their architecture. Reinforced buttresses along the front sheltered the entire outer landing with concrete pillars and protective walls. Heavy metal doors and bulletproof glass inlays protected the main entrance. A small band of armed men could hold off an army from these ramparts. I imagined myself ascending the staircase of a Mayan Temple as we climbed up to the doors. At the top, Gabriel pulled one open and we stepped into the foyer. I peeked through the glass on the second set of doors before stepping into the lobby. Interior security cameras captured our images as we entered the screening area. A courteous but authoritarian type female security guard asked me to state my business. Her matronly appearance with brown hair, round face and frigid frown signaled us we were in for a more thorough search than the airport. Her former occupation could have been that of an East Berlin Border Guard. She inspected our identifications and led us to a magnetometer to check for weapons. Upon completion, another security official told us to be seated in the deserted lobby. As the uniformed woman walked to the far end of the lobby, a receptionist sat behind a thick window, I presumed of bulletproof glass.

"We don't get many walk-in visitors here. An agent on the floor will see you shortly," the lieutenant announced from his post.

This must be what suspects experience, I thought. I checked my watch three times in 20 minutes wondering if time had stopped. The longer one was made to wait, the more one felt like an intruder. I was about to leave when a lean man in a suit stepped into the lobby from a door next to the reception window. The business type figure walked past us and went directly to the security station. Following a brief conversation, he approached us.

"Mr. Freiderich, come with me."

Gabriel and I followed him into a 10-by-10 interview room. He swiped his card to gain access. Once inside, he offered a seat at an oak table across from him. A mirrored window shouted that others might be watching.

"I'm Special Agent Dobbins. How may I help you?"

Painstakingly, I recited exactly what I had told Jay. The agent struggled to suppress a yawn throughout our saga. He seemed equally unimpressed with my credentials or request for assistance. Upon finishing, I added, "*and they illegally entered your country and may be part of a larger plot to attack the United States.*" Agent Dobbins jotted down a few notes.

His closing statement confirmed what his inattentiveness told me, "With all due respect to your position and rank, do you realize how many of these alleged terrorist plots we get every day? We do, however, appreciate your coming, and please, keep us informed."

Baffled, I asked, "Do you not share intelligence on terrorists?"

"Yes, but not classified information. Incidentally, do you have a photo of the missing person?"

"Not with me. My photos are at the hotel. I am certain because our Intelligence Unit already provided copies to law enforcement agencies, including the FBI."

"We prefer to have originals. Give me your address. One of our agents will pick them up to save you a trip. If anything new develops, contact this office." He handed me his business card as we returned to the lobby.

"We are staying at the Holiday Inn on this street. Thank you for speaking with us. I hope we find these young men soon enough to prevent something terrible from happening."

"So do I," the agent added. We shook hands and concluded our business. Dobbins pointed to the guards, who escorted us from the building.

Through the bitter wind, I walked silently back to our hotel. My hope had changed to despair. While the agent was polite, his tenor was placating, if not disconcerting. Gabriel's words interrupted my thoughts, "I think they will do nothing. We had better call your friend as soon as we return. As the Americans say, '*He blew you off!*'" I patted Gabriel on the shoulder.

My first direct contact with the FBI left me feeling foolish. At first, I harbored the notion that my case may be of no interest to them, that I was *a nobody*. At that point, I lamented valuable time had been wasted. These people seem to proclaim a policy of cooperation with law enforcement, yet their conversation suspiciously flowed one-way. This international police agency left me wondering whether this was the proper approach.

3 | ETHNIC FEELINGS

"Jay?"

"Yes?"

"I went to the FBI as you suggested and they *blew me off*!"

"Right after you left, it dawned on me that might happen," Jay offered.

"The agent told me to report my missing nephew to the police. Is this the correct procedure?"

"Well, he's not missing from here. Besides, he's an adult. Sorry for the wild goose chase. The FBI dumps a lot of referrals on us, unless they can grab favorable press. Did they seem interested in anything you told them?"

"I found Agent Dobbins difficult to read. I am disappointed. I feel I must not turn over the photos, but this would be counterproductive."

"How many photos do you have?" Jay asked.

"Seven. This includes Jusef, Ali and five other young Arab males, three of whom met Ali in Hamburg. I believe they are members of the same terrorist cell due to the fact their departures from Germany were all in close proximity. We tracked five traveling to Mexico about the time we discovered Jusef and Ali on their way to Canada."

"I don't see what else you could have done," Jay responded.

"When he first came to Germany, I drove Jusef to my sister Sonja's apartment in Cologne. He told me he was glad to leave the horror and destruction of Baghdad, but he never said anything to make me suspicious."

"What's the story on this Ali kid? How does he fit into all this?"

"My sister Kristina and her husband were good friends with his family. The young man's parents were killed during one of the bombings over Baghdad. He had no one else who to take him in. After arriving in Hamburg, Ali never surfaced again. So, have you any suggestions?"

There was a moment of silence. "Let me pass on this information to a colleague of mine. His name is Bill. He's damn good at connecting the dots. "

I sent Gabriel for lunch to allow myself a moment to think. Had I overlooked something important? In considering past events and the last person who had seen Ali, I reflected back to two days before the family reunion in Istria, Croatia.

My two nephews and I walked through drizzle along a tree-lined street in Piran. We strolled past neighborhood pubs with wooden signs hanging from ornamental ironwork, awning-covered antique stores and ice cream shops. I recall the aroma of freshly baked bread had tempted our senses outside the bakery even before seeing the pastries in the front window. A butcher shop displayed their best cuts of pork, lamb and chicken along with fresh sausages. We arrived at Café al Arabesque, one of the most popular spots of Piran.

Contrasting green hills hovered over the town's uniformly red tiled roofs on top of the Balkan stone houses. Miniature stone castles, winding stairways, cobble-stoned streets, and gothic turrets covered with multi-colored pennants beckoned visitors up from the sea. Piran was our usual stop off before Aunt Katrina and Uncle Fritz's farm.

Secretly, I was glad Ali had not come to the family picnic. Jusef told me his friend was busy with studies at university. Now that I had thought about it, I could not recall anyone but medical students studying day and night. Had he come to the family reunion, I would have asked him about his studies.

We laughed about Uncle Joe and my nephew's boyhood memories as we walked. Joe was always tiring us with history lessons on German folklore and lyrics. He seemed to be an expert on all matters of German origin.

As we stepped into the Arabesque, we encountered a man made fog of cigarette smoke. Some indulged on a variety of herbal teas, while snacking on a rainbow of pastries from the bakery across the street. Coffee and sweet mint tea helped start our morning and relieve the chill.

At first, the mix of German and Arab seemed complacent to the news as they sipped coffee. Three elevated flat screen televisions sat on wooden shelves in the crowded café announcing the morning news in Arabic with German subtitles. No one paid particular attention to the announcer. Each patron was ignoring the day's broadcast: '*Political refugees will now be asked to return to the country of their homeland once the federal law goes into effect next week...*'

Gabriel poked at my rib with his elbow. "Look, there is Uncle Joe. Who is the old man sitting with him?"

"Where?" I asked, looking across the smoke-filled room.

"Over there in the corner by the window." Gabriel pointed at the stout bald man with wire-rimmed glasses. We waved, and Joe waved back. I was not in the mood to listen to his ranting about government conspiracies.

Now I remember: Gabriel asked Jusef if he was sure his friend could come. Jusef repeated his initial response that Ali was busy with his studies. Nevertheless, Gabriel insisted he was certain he waved at a man standing by the window, thinking at the time that he had seen Ali. I also remembered that Gabriel said the individual whom he thought to be Ali had hurried away.

Moments later, Jusef left our table, presumably to use the restroom. About that time, Uncle Joe caught my attention a second time. Consequently, my other nephew and I made our way to his far-corner table. Joe introduced us to his white-haired friend, Hans Gruber, a veteran of the eleventh Panzer Division.

"This is my great nephew, Gabriel, and my sister's son, Thomas. He is an important investigator in charge of Hamburg Police."

"Yours must be an interesting job, keeping an eye on everyone," Hans added as he extended his oversized hand.

While Uncle Joe adjusted his glasses, he casually asked, "Thomas, are you expecting someone to join you today?"

"No. Why do you ask?"

"Just wondering. I saw Jusef speaking to a young man outside, right there," pointing as he spoke.

I looked out the window. There was no one there. I remember patting Uncle Joe on his shoulder, and thanking him for being so concerned. Inside, I dismissed the matter as just another one of his conspiracy theories. Maybe I should have taken him seriously.

They accepted my offer to pick up their guest check. When Gabriel and I returned to our table, Jusef was already seated. I scrutinized his wet hair and jacket. Following my glance, Jusef looked down at his sleeve.

"I apologize for my dishonesty. I never went to the restroom. I was outside smoking a cigarette, and did not want you to know I smoked."

"By the way, Jusef, are you sure your friend Ali will be unable to join us for the family reunion?" I asked.

"I am positive. He is at school, and cannot come."

"The only reason I mentioned this was Uncle Joe thought he saw you and Ali outside."

"Impossible, a stranger lit a cigarette for me. Besides, he has never seen Ali."

The noisy television in the corner announced, "*Sixteen members of the Palestinian Jihad were killed today in the West Bank town of Hebron.*" Another news item was reported from Al' Jazeera: "*In*

Palestine, freedom fighters stood up to the tanks of the Imperial Army!"
The scene depicted teenagers throwing stones at Israeli armored
vehicles.

Rashid Hamadi, the café owner, bellowed out his opinion to
the patrons from behind the counter, "*Does anyone care? Can they
even make them human? If twenty dogs died today, do we want to know if
they were poodles or their gender—but people? Were they young, old, men
or women—they are someone's family members, are they not?*"

Out of the corner of my eye, I noticed Jusef's sympathy, along
with several Arab patrons. No doubt, he compared the Palestinians
plight to the occupation of his hometown, Baghdad.

I also noticed Hans Gruber looking at Hamadi. He stood up,
moved with what he observed and commented to the owner, "I
was there when our panzers suppressed the uprising in the Warsaw
Ghetto. I am saddened to think people have learned nothing."

The television news of the day shifted to the insurrection in
Iraq: "*Today, another year has past since the occupation in Iraq began.
A bomb in the temporary American Embassy killed dozens of workers…now that 130,000 occupation troops are battling; insurgents remain
in only two cities of Iraq.*"

Hamadi commented, "I remember Bush saying America is
not into *Nation Building.*"

An anonymous voice from across the room shouted, "You
mean *Empire Building!*"

Shaking his finger at the screen, Hamadi continued, "Where
is the outrage over this?"

Demonstrating crowds of youths came in view of news cameras in Islamabad with shouts of: *Kill the Jews; Kill the British; Kill
the Americans.* I noticed some people around us reacting to the
broadcast, grumbling and murmuring. Some stood up, angrily
shouting at the TV. I felt uneasy and signaled Gabriel time to leave
by a nudge on the arm.

4 | FAMILY REUNION

THE EVENT STARTED PLEASANTLY ENOUGH. MY PARENTS SEEMED to enjoy the drive in the rented van through mountainous terrain along narrow roadways that occasionally funneled into one-lane passages. The VW's engine struggled to reach our journey's highest points just below rugged peaks. We continued past each vista overlooking alpine forests, rugged outcroppings and pastoral valley. Changes in altitude and the crisp air put my 70-year-old father to sleep. Just a few years earlier, he had served as our official family chauffeur.

Lightheartedly, I hinted, "He could not stay awake as long this trip."

That was my mother's unofficial signal to speak. "Since he retired from his medical practice, your father has slowed down. He no longer prefers to walk with me. I am no spring chicken, but he is only eight years older. He stares at the TV all day in a zombie trance, slouching in his leather chair. The man retired before his time. He had a few good years left as a psychiatrist, but refused to keep up with the politically correct methods and simply quit. I fear he has given up on life."

Looking in the mirror, I analyzed my silver-haired, slender father, curled up with eyeglasses still on top of his head. Would

I be him in 30 years, losing social contacts, disinterested in the world, waiting for life to end between commercials?

My response was apologetic, "I have few regrets in my life except letting you both down by not following in father's footsteps."

Her stern gaze signaled she was ready to launch into her usual litany of complaints. "Your father was more disappointed in your sisters for marrying those foreigners. Look how they turned out. Sonja's husband is trapped in Iraq and Kristina is now a widow. She dropped out of university when she was pregnant by that Mohammed. At least she was proud enough to be ashamed of her situation. She did not have to go to Iraq. I would have helped her out."

I glanced at her with disapproval.

Ignoring me, her words poured out in machine gun fashion, "Having both of my grandsons the same age was a bit awkward considering the difference in age of my daughters…and when the youngest, Kristina, married an Iraqi, we were not even invited to her In-Law's wedding reception. Do you realize Jusef was never baptized? What can Kristina do now without a formal education? What will become of my grandchildren? They do not fit here or there. They have mixed blood, a sin from their parents."

I wanted to say 'pray for us,' but instead responded, "Mama, calm down. All this is not so bad. Everything will be okay."

She returned to her litany. "And you, his only son; he disapproved when you joined the military. Your decision to enter the police service devastated him. You totally disappointed him when you did not resume your studies. However, your successful career has made him your number one fan. He constantly boasts of his son Thomas. If your name appears in the paper, or God forbid, throwing her hands above her head, is shown on television, his friends avoid him for days."

The time had come to go on the offense, "Mother, how do you feel about us?"

"I love all of my children and grandchildren equally. Did I not teach every one of you to read music and play an instrument?"

"Yes, but you loved music."

Irritated, she tilted her seat back, folded her arms, closed her eyes and feigned sleep to avoid my questions. Mother's strong will was concealed by her petite frame, graying blonde hair, attractive face, complimented by a youthful complexion. Eventually, she drifted into a slumber and complete silence for the next few hours, forcing me to turn off the radio.

As the van rolled across the old wooden bridge, each oak plank made its own familiar click-clack alarm, announcing our arrival and startling my parents awake. The noise alerted the two watchdogs, one white and one black German Sheppard, both springing up from their nap in the sun. Their bark brought Uncle Fritz and Aunt Katrina from their gingerbread farmhouse protected by its copper roof. They greeted us with hugs and steins of beer.

As my mother rubbed her eyes, she looked out over the green hills and open pastures, divided by a serpentine wall of stone in the distance. "Now I remember how beautiful this country is when we visit. This long trip is always worthwhile."

Dad inhaled the pure mountain air as he stretched. Looking around at the other cars, he exclaimed, "Oh! Uncle Joe is here; you cannot miss that shiny red 1968 Beetle." He smirked then looked at mama slyly from the corner of his eye, "Your brother keeps his old car in perfect condition."

Ignoring his comments, my mother asked, "Where are Sonja and the boys?"

"Sonja is in the kitchen. Jusef and Gabriel are setting up the stage and picnic area. Thomas, go and check on them."

Mother quietly turned to Katrina, "I hope he does not start his inspection ritual."

Katrina declared, "I shall break that stupid monocle if he begins checking my clean dishes."

Mother laughed, "He uses a magnifying glass, not a monocle. I will see that he puts his glass away." Pointing in admiration at the olive grove, she changed the subject, "These trees remind me of the good times here. I can picture Gabriel and Jusef walking through the trees with their fathers."

Katrina concurred, "We have always been happy to host our entire family on these ten hectares as a neutral site during these days of difficult travel. We believe ethnic and religious differences can be overcome if everyone would only take care of the land and help their neighbors. Our extended family has inhabited this land for over a century. These olive gardens were planted by Romans more than a thousand years ago and worked by pagans, Christians and Muslims for centuries. Good caretakers are all the earth needs to sustain us for generations, according to God's plan."

While my mother and aunt returned to the kitchen, father and I set out to observe the others. Jusef and Gabriel were busy lifting beer kegs into half barrels of ice, inserting taps and sampling as they went. The band wore traditional costumes of lederhosen and brightly embroidered red vests. Uncle Joe was dressed in his Alpine outfit, complete with a hat covered in pins and badges from past festivals and clubs. He sat with a drummer, a keyboard player, a clarinetist, two horn players and his premier zither expert, each member ready to perform. Joe sat on a bench with the older musicians, while the others gathered around the younger electric keyboard player to tune up between beers.

On cue, Uncle Fritz gave the signal to begin and the band burst into a march tempo. At the same time, an entourage of women followed Aunt Katrina from the house to rows of picnic tables. They carried trays of ham, home made sausage and roast beef, while my mother and Sonja trailed behind them with salads, fresh breads and desserts. The women systematically arranged treats of apple, cherry and apricot strudels, chocolate cake, fruit, and pies on the center table, adorned with hand-embroidered tablecloths.

Uncle Fritz had converted a workbench that served as a bar stocked with extra mugs and glasses, bottles of schnapps, whiskey, vodka, wine, brandy and cognac. My nephews strategically positioned kegs of beer at opposite ends of the tables with a third keg near the stage. Fritz gestured an okay sign to the boys.

Under the October sky, our reunion had turned into a family festival, beginning with the children dancing and adults singing. Music began to draw them into the picnic area as old friends and relatives collected in their usual nesting spots. Dancers whirled and twirled faster and faster while some at the tables started singing. The more they drank, the more people joined in the festivities. The crowd sang louder and louder, each verse with more passion.

As generations mingled, old and young shared the moment. A few outlying elders seated near the bonfire launched directly into storytelling and tales of their ancestors. Folklore and music took a big part of what they brought to the table. Another chapter was forged in our family history.

While not all participated in the festivities, those who did were renewing family bonds. Mohammed and Assam's absence left only Jusef and Gabriel to represent the eastern heritage of the family. For the moment, family differences were forgotten.

From the time everyone arrived, our family musicians pounded out a rhythmic beat, while I sat across from Sonja and my family at the table. Our conversation was not the usual politics or gossip. She remarked how the full harvest moon coming into view cast shadows of light and dark on the rugged mountaintops and silver valleys. I added that a harvest celebration was not complete without the hillside fragrances of freshly cut wheat. My sister and I took in the sound of clapping hands and tapping feet echoing throughout the hills.

I was pleased at how everyone was joining in. Some guests began pounding fists on picnic tables with others stomping feet to the music. Several revelers jumped up onto the tables, shouting and screaming. At the same time, accordion, brass and drum music came together in a crescendo. Even the band members rocked the worn wooden stage in full motion.

Sonja asked me, "The platform appears ready to collapse any moment. Do you think they are safe?"

"They use the same stage every year. Everything will work out. Calm down and have a drink," I suggested.

"Ugh, that is all you guys know," she said, storming away.

Uncle Joe, the partly bald, red-faced accordion player was standing toward the back corner of the band. Jusef surprised him when he picked up a 1920s button box off to the side of the stage. Immediately, a frown appeared on Joe's face, watching the young artist manhandle his prized instrument.

"Be careful; that is a family heirloom," Joe barked.

"May I have a try?" Jusef pointed to the button box, then to himself. Reluctantly, Uncle Joe nodded his approval to appease the crowd. Jusef's grandmother had introduced him to the concertina and his mother encouraged him to continue to play the instrument after they moved away from Europe. His grandmother's approving smile was noticeable to everyone, especially Joe.

The band broke into a familiar folk tune. Joe and his band members burst into song. Those who knew the words sang along while the others hummed, while others sang along 'la la la.' Everyone clasped arms and swayed side to side.

Sonja hugged me, "Tommie, do you wish every day could be like this? If only Assam and Kristina were here, things would be perfect."

"Speaking of perfect, look over there," I pointed at two completely mismatched dance partners in their seventies.

Tall, slender, Aunt Inga with bright yellow hair wore a red dress with matching shoes and lipstick. She was on the dance floor with Otto, her brother-in-law, an entire head shorter in stature, balding, belly hanging enough to conceal his buckle and half his belt between his white shirt and black pants. She dragged him in a swirling motion around the floor, while his shuffling feet struggled to follow. Swaying and twirling with arching movements, she occasionally dipped back deeply, bringing one knee to her torso, kicking her leg high into the air while clinging to Otto. The entire family applauded, including Inga's husband Karl, who anchored himself to a table close to a beer keg.

Uncle Joe's fingers struggled over the keys of his accordion, trying to keep up with Jusef's quickened pace. The crowd applauded as Jusef danced wildly in circles around the stage, moving and playing faster as the tempo increased. Joe attempted to belt out his own melody as Jusef repeatedly bumped him, putting him off balance, pushing him further to the edge of the rocking stage. Joe desperately clutched his accordion as his legs began to wobble. Defensively backing to the rear corner to avoid Jusef, beads of beer sweat flowed off his forehead.

Jusef's last bump launched Joe off the back of the wooden platform over the side of the mountain. The assailant leaped from the stage into the enthusiastic crowd. Overcome by the crowd's noise, the startled cry for help accompanied the last squeal of the old timer's music box had gone unnoticed.

Someone from the crowd clapped and screamed, "Excellent, excellent; we are all family!"

Several meters below, the battered figure lay on his side, propped up on one elbow. Joe slowly stood up, brushed himself off and started back up the hill on all fours, accordion in tow. Out of the darkness, his attention was drawn to two men's voices on the moonlit hillside.

Sonja interrupted my dance. "You must stop Gabriel and Jusef. They are both drunk and making fools of themselves. Did you see Jusef jump into the crowd? Please, stop them before someone breaks his neck!"

She pointed to her son dancing on the tabletop with three girls, two blondes and a brunette. The girls took turns goosing Gabriel to see him jump while he did his best to avoid spilling any beer. Sonja's face displayed serious concern.

"Let him dance. You worry too much. He looks fine to me," I reassured.

Jusef and Uncle Joe disappeared. Both were missing when I scanned the tabletops to survey the crowd. After a few minutes, I left to find them.

"Help," a faint voice called from the dark. "Help me! I am down here."

That sounded like Uncle Joe. I explored the edge of the mountainside. Looking down, I spotted him crawling up the hill and rushed to assist.

"Thank God, you found me."

"What the hell happened?"

"Jusef pushed me off the stage. This was no accident."

"Are you hurt?"

"I am okay. Well, at least I can walk. Still, I say he knocked me down the hill on purpose. Then they refused to help me."

"—They? Who?"

"Jusef and his friend; you know, the one I told you about. I called out to them and they ran away and hid."

"Who was with Jusef?"

"That same one I saw outside the Café yesterday."

"You mean, Ali?"

"I do not know his name. I never saw him before yesterday. They are up to something. Nothing good comes from secret meetings."

As we continued back up the hillside another 15 meters, Joe brushed off soil from his knees. The moment he had re-established his footing, he pulled away from me, indicating he could make the rest of the distance without my assistance. As I reached for his accordion, he snatched his instrument away, but said nothing further. Aside from his disheveled appearance and minor bruises, the only serious impact was a damaged ego.

Once we reached the top, I was satisfied that he and his accordion were okay. I found my uncle a steady chair and a fresh beer. Turning my attention from my uncle back to my nephew, I decided to look for Jusef.

I motioned Gabriel to return from the dance floor. "Have you seen Jusef?" I asked.

"I saw him about twenty minutes ago over there," Gabriel pointed in the direction of the far corner of the stage.

"Was he alone?"

"I think so, why?"

"Have you any idea where he went?"

"No, but I can help you search." With that, we headed in the opposite directions.

A few minutes later, Gabriel found Jusef standing by some parked vehicles, and called out, "Jusef, Uncle Thomas is looking for you."

"Leave me alone."

"Why did you push Uncle Joe?" Gabriel challenged Jusef. "What is wrong with you; are you crazy?"

Jusef shouted back, "You fool! We are the outsiders here. The Germans will never accept either of us. I will not participate in this charade any longer. These people killed my father and our grandfather. The time of revenge for our oppressed people has come. As an Arab, your duty is to join us."

"I am no terrorist!"

"Neither are we. We are freedom fighters. You and I share the same blood and you cannot turn your back on our heritage. So, are you to be trusted?" Jusef challenged.

"You are the one who is fooling himself. You are blind; they have been using you. Once you obey their commands, they will discard you like human waste."

"Get out of my way," Jusef said, starting for the woods.

Gabriel grabbed his arm. Jusef swiveled around, slugging the side of Gabriel's head with his fist. Another blow immediately followed and Gabriel struggled to remain on his feet. A swift kick to Gabriel's midsection left him breathless, and sent him to the ground. As he tried to lift himself up, his assailant threw a right hook that caught him squarely in the face. Blood gushed from his nose and sent him back to the ground.

"Jusef, hurry up. We must leave at once," an Arab voice called out from the edge of the wooded area.

Jusef looked down at Gabriel, not as a cousin. He delivered a final kick to Gabriel's face, causing him to rollover in pain, nearly losing consciousness. Within moments, Jusef had disappeared into a veil of darkness.

5 | FORCES OF GOOD AND EVIL

Jay asked me to meet him at the Justice Center. We went to the second floor and knocked on an orange door. The sign read, *Commanding Officer - Narcotics Unit - Lieutenant William Popovich.* Bill unlocked the door, and invited us in. Jay introduced me as a colleague from Hamburg. For the next 45 minutes, I updated Bill on my dilemma.

"We thought you could help find his other nephew, Jusef," Jay began.

Bill turned toward me, and asked, "What makes you think he's *still in Cleveland?*"

"Ten days ago, I learned that Jusef sent a message from University Circle to his mother." Jay's friend sat across from me patiently listening with a stone face. After a prolonged silent pause, I continued, "You might think this is crazy, but I think Jusef has become involved with a group of terrorists who are going to attack your country. I want to find him before he can do anything foolish."

Bill raised his hand as if he was stopping traffic. He pointed his finger at me and asked, "Does anyone know what you're doing here?"

"My superiors have approved an unofficial investigation into this matter. Naturally, they are being kept informed."

Bill returned a dark stare. Possibly he was analyzing my story and situation. Then again, perhaps he was thinking about how *not* to get involved. Police work can be challenging at times, especially when there are rivaling jurisdictions. For several moments, I entertained the suspicion that Jay's friend was toying with the idea of looking for a plausible excuse—a way out.

"Thomas is convinced the FBI blew him off this morning," Jay's comment breaking the silence.

For the first time, Bill's face cracked an impish smile. "That smells familiar. Okay, let me see those photos," he beckoned with his index finger.

With a measure of relief, I retrieved the photos from my breast pocket and turned them over. "One more thing, my assistant, Karl informed me that several generic messages have been sent from a Baghdad mosque to various Acme offices in Germany, Canada and America. Gentlemen, what do you suppose this means? The message announced '*everything is in place*.' What alarms me is there has been no terrorist activity, almost as if they have taken a holiday. Are they ready to strike?"

Bill's eyes searched the ceiling as if the hidden meaning was floating somewhere above the room. "So, you think this could be the big bang? Some sort of Tet Offensive?"

"I suspect that is the case, and time is of the essence."

Gabriel's eyes widened. Not until this moment had he realized the gravity of the situation. I had not shared the full depth of my suspicions to avoid overly upsetting him.

"We do not have all the facts, only that my cousin is involved with a group that may do terrible things. My uncle has been doing his best to prevent a disaster," my young protégé proposed.

"Have a seat," Bill offered. "Why are you bringing this to me?"

"Jay recommended you to us," I said.

I caught Bill's brief disapproving glance focused at Jay.

Jay defended his position, "Thomas is my friend. I've known his family for years. He usually stays at my house whenever he is in town. I believe the German police have discovered some kind of plot, or he wouldn't be here. He needs your help."

"Help? How?" Bill quizzed.

"You have resources. Your narcs and their spies are everywhere."

"They're informants, not spies." Bill leaned forward in his chair.

Jay replied, "Don't be so sensitive. They'll always be a bunch of rats to me."

"Some are, but we need them to do what we do," Bill stated.

"I understand your position, Lieutenant. My work in Germany is quite similar," I noted.

"For the record, have you reported any of these facts or suspicions to the CIA, the FBI or Homeland Security?" Bill inquired.

"We have been monitoring developments for some time in Germany. As a result, we informed your FBI and State Department, but they seem to be preoccupied with other matters. As of this morning, at Jay's suggestion, I contacted your local FBI office."

"So they are investigating," Bill concluded.

"Not exactly."

"What do you mean?"

"An agent reluctantly took down our suspicions and descriptions on a yellow note pad, and told me that someone would contact me. I explained how inquiries had been made through my own police department in Hamburg as to the progress on information we furnished the FBI in Germany weeks ago. To date, we hear nothing. All the FBI will tell us is that the matter is under investigation. This is why we have come to you."

His face belied his amusement, "Your situation has a well-known ring. Okay, let me see your surveillance photos, and please point out the cast of characters." He scrutinized the photos from Airport Security in Slovenia and Hamburg, while I proceeded to point out Jusef, Ali and the unknown suspects. "I can keep these?" he asked.

"Yes, we have duplicates."

"Okay, I'll see if we can find any of your needles in our haystack. Where can you be reached?" Bill asked as he stood up to escort us toward the door.

I informed him that my nephew and I were registered at the Holiday Inn Lakeside. Once we left Bill's office, Jay went back to work, while Gabriel and I returned to the hotel for an early dinner. After the meal, we retired to our room.

The evening news consisted of mindless chatter, interrupted by babbling commercials. I pressed the mute button in an attempt to focus my attention on the soundless screen, hoping to see Jusef's image. I was a spectator to murder, arson and political ramblings along with more annoying commercials.

Finally, a news report caught my attention, so I reactivated the sound. The latest murder in a spree of crimes against Arab storeowners revealed that each of the victims had been killed on the east side. What occurred to me was just about this time, Jusef and his friends would have arrived in Cleveland.

While Aunt Katrina took over Uncle Joe's care at a picnic table out of harm's way, I continued my search. Coming upon a bloody Gabriel, curled up on the ground by the woods, I learned of his assault after carrying him back to Aunt Katrina's first aid table.

"What happened? Were you pushed down the hill, too?" Uncle Joe quizzed.

"Worse than that, I found Jusef. He demanded I go with him and Ali on a secret mission. When I refused to participate, he attacked me and ran off with his friend."

"I knew there was a third man! That boy is evil," he self-righteously proclaimed.

Aunt Katrina continued attending to the wounded.

Gabriel concluded, "Jusef has never been violent. Someone has trained my cousin to fight like an assassin."

I made another note for later: Messages to Baghdad Mosque from outside must be checked; my investigators must search Ali's apartment in Hamburg. If this is a secret organization, they have a very clever way of operating.

Another transmission:

"From: Acme, Inc., Region 5 Office
Project Manager
To: All Offices
Project commencing soon in Region 5. Send all personnel and any additional equipment. Funding for projects coming in on schedule."

The Lizard instructed Yassar to take the usual precautions in picking the two young men arriving from Canada. They were scheduled to arrive on the return trip from Windsor Casino. The smuggling procedure involved the purchase of round-trip chartered bus tickets for a daylong gambling junket. Once on the Canadian side, the two departing soldiers would switch both identities and jackets, allowing the two new arrivals their reserved seats on the bus returning to Cleveland. Their bus was scheduled to arrive at a nearly deserted parking lot shortly after 11 o'clock.

As the male passengers stepped off the bus, Yassar studied each one. He watched for two wearing Brown's jackets with matching headgear. While other passengers headed toward their vehicles, Jusef and Ali stood around not sure what to expect next. All they had been told was to stay close to where the bus dropped them and that someone from Acme would meet them. Yassar waited several minutes to satisfy himself that the two new arrivals had not be followed before restarting the car and driving toward them.

"Do you have the time?" he asked in Arabic.

"Sir, are you from Acme?" Ali responded.

Yassar reached across the front seat and opened the car door. "I am Yassar. Welcome to Cleveland." During the final leg of their lengthy trip, the large man in his mid forties would speak no further.

En route to their destination, Yassar drove evasively: He turned down several side streets and drove through alleys to ensure no one was following. He drove the route as if he had taken this trip before. The 20-minute ride ended when Yassar turned off West 25th Street and into a storefront parking lot and proceeded to the rear of an aging two-story brick structure and stopped abruptly. The space was squeezed between a row of neglected houses to their left and an old apartment building straight ahead.

Yassar motioned with his head for the two young men to follow him, and proceeded to enter the building through the delivery door. Their driver unlocked the rear steel-door, and gestured with his hand for Ali and Jusef to come. They entered a dimly lit, windowless storage room filled with stacked blue-plastic crates and cases of beer and pop.

Yassar pointed toward a short stack of empty crates, "Sit. Mr. Lazar will be with you shortly." He folded his arms and stood before the only visible exit. At no time did he pick up a telephone or leave the room to tell anyone of their arrival.

The new recruits sat in silence, watching Yassar, wondering who Lazar was and how long they would be forced to wait. As the minutes ticked away, they grew more uncomfortable. Constant clicking of a thermostat caused the temperature to remain at 78 degrees. Whoever Lazar was, these conditions sent the message he was in control.

Yassar, too, felt the heat and casually removed and hung his jacket on a hook next to the exit without removing his black leather gloves. With his arms refolded as a sentry, the tall man stood guard over them. Observing their growing impatience, he granted his permission, "You may remove your jackets while we wait."

The silence of the room was in sharp contrast to the constant wailing of passing sirens outside, as if they had never left Baghdad. Could the attack already have started? Another siren screeched by. Are we in the middle of the fighting? Moreover, where is Lazar? Convinced the attack on the Americans had already begun, Ali suspected they were being held in reserve.

Their speculative thoughts came to an abrupt end when the door at the opposite end of the room swung open. A silhouette emerged from the shadows, revealing a man wearing a fisherman's sweater. He came to the center of the room, and reached up to pull the chain that turned on a shaded single bulb overhead at eye level, illuminating the immediate area below.

Yassar snapped to attention, "Good evening Mr. Lazar. How are you?"

"I am fine." He turned toward Ali and Jusef, and inquired in Arabic, "And how are our two guests tonight?"

"Fine, sir," they jointly choired in shaky voices, as they hastily rose to their feet.

"And who do I have the pleasure of meeting?" Lazar requested in a formal and commanding tone. He inspected the new arrivals as if they were part of his military recruits.

"I am Jusef Müeller, and this is my friend, Ali Mohammed."

"Those were your names in Canada. Here you are Pierre Monet and Robert Claret from Cleveland, Ohio."

Lazar withdrew two driver licenses from his shirt pocket. A photo was already on each license. "Here are your new documents. Let me have your other papers." They removed what was in their wallets, and handed everything over to Lazar, their identities replaced with new ones.

The faceless voice asked from the shadows, "Did you encounter any problems during your journey?"

Ali responded first, "No sir, all went well. There were no difficulties."

Jusef nervously prattled, "My family was becoming suspicious; good thing we left on the night of the family reunion. I would not be missed until the following day. We departed Croatia on a flight to Montreal, using the passports and credit cards that were provided to us. After we arrived in Montreal, we were driven to Windsor and told to stay in the Casino until contacted. Two men from Cleveland met us in the restaurant, and we exchanged identification and credit cards. They escorted us to their returning bus and that is how we arrived."

"And you are sure there were no problems at the border?"

"No-sir."

Lazar leaned forward. For the first time, his facial features came into view. He cocked his head and two cold black eyes shot through Jusef. "You-are-sure?"

"Yes, sir. The border guards entered our bus and did not check us. The driver turned on the cabin lights and we pretended to be sleeping like all the other passengers. The man requested photo identification, and all the passengers held up their drivers licenses at the same time. He welcomed us to the U.S. and departed."

"Did anyone follow you?"

"I do not think so. We spoke to no one." Jusef flashed a worried glance to Ali.

"You do not *think* so?"

"Your driver took a very unusual route. He made several twists and turns. If anyone did follow us, your driver lost them."

Without comment, Yassar looked at Lazar and nodded.

"Tonight, you will stay here. A lot is at stake. Do you have any questions?" Lazar asked.

"Why did we leave our identification and credit cards with the men in Windsor?" Jusef asked.

Lazar left the room.

Jusef turned to Yassar. "Did I say something wrong?"

"You talked too much. Those men will be using your credit cards to create the illusion that you are still in Canada. We will set up cots, one for each of us. Now, I must go and secure the door."

Following Lazar's departure, Yassar reached up and darkened the room and left.

Jusef switched to speaking French with the hope that Yassar didn't *par le la France.* "You think we have done the right thing?" Jusef whispered. Ali did not answer. "What I mean is, do you think coming here to attack the Americans is a good idea?"

Ali returned, "Shh!"

"Why have we not been told our purpose? Are we to become martyrs for the cause?"

Ali responded, "Allah is on our side, no matter what is asked of us. I am ready to make the ultimate sacrifice. For you, training was only an adventure, a game with interesting scenarios. Now we are here to strike the enemy on his home ground. This is the real thing. Some will die; maybe one of us."

Jusef continued in French, "Was Gabriel right? Are we just pawns in a worldwide struggle?"

Ali reassured Jusef, "Gabriel is not Arab. Allah gives you the ability to follow His will. Everything works out. Have faith, praise be to Allah. Ask Him for courage to do your duty without fear or reservation."

The pounding at the front door alerted Yassar their breakfast had arrived. An olive skinned man in his twenties entered after Yassar removed a long 2 by 4 from its brackets and opened the door. The day manager readjusted the aged yellowing cardboard signs with ghostly letters blocking the view through the front windows. He carried four white paper bags to the back and placed the fast food on a well-worn butcher-block table. "Eat up. We have an hour before I open the store."

The manager offered to shake hands, "My name is Sam—" Yassar's disapproving stare reminded him about the rule. He stopped instantly withdrawing his hand. Yassar turned to Jusef and Ali, busily devouring their food, "We do not use names here!" Sam turned immediately and went back to the front of the building to ready the store for business.

Following their brief meal, Yassar instructed Jusef and Ali to carry bundles of newspapers from an overstuffed van parked behind the store. They piled bundles in front of three elderly women wearing burkas. They were seated around a table, scissors in hand, removing the coupon sections from the stacked newspapers that were placed beside them.

"What are they doing?" Jusef inquired.

Sam hesitated and lowered his voice, "They cut out coupons and sort them accordingly to earn money from vendors who redeem them. We use the money to fund our cause, both here and overseas. This is repeated across the country, generating thousands and possibly millions of dollars. Our funding comes from food stamps and coupons, not products. No one checks store sales records. Our customers exchange food stamps for cash. All of this is how the Americans help us fund our war against them."

The Internal Revenue Service saw Lazar as just another inner city struggling merchant. A chain of stores looked like separate units owned by individual storekeepers barely surviving in the poorest parts of Cleveland. Lazar capitalized on this image using the tax code that allows immigrant businessmen a seven-year tax exemption to shelter his income. On the surface, Lazar's enterprises appeared to be within the law, while government programs for food stamps and low-income housing provided his operation with a reliable source of revenue and loyal clients.

Yassar chauffeured Jusef and Ali across town to the Cedar store. Behind his closed manager's office door, Lazar was on his cell phone, operating a bill counter at the same time. When the amount surpassed $20,000.00 in twenty-dollar denominations, he knew this had been a good day for a struggling merchant.

Lazar emerged from his office to greet the arrivals with, "How is everyone this evening?"

He clasped his hands together in a polite gesture as Yassar, Jusef and Ali walked into the back room of the store. The surroundings were similar but larger than the other location.

"Fine, sir," Ali said.

"Sit down. I have a few more questions," Lazar said. They nodded in agreement. "Are you familiar with C4?"

"Yes, that is the primary one that we have been instructed in," Ali replied.

"Excellent. How much training did you receive in the use of blasting caps and remote controlled detonations?"

"We received thorough training with blasting caps but very little about remote devices," Jusef said.

"So you know how to set the charges and place them appropriately. Shall I say you need more training with remote control devices?"

"Yes," they jointly answered. Jusef grasped the words remote control had implied he might not be called to martyrdom. He gave a brief sigh of relief.

Lizard picked up on Jusef's sigh. "I see you agree with my methods. Although suicide bombers are necessary in some cases, this is not the only strategy."

Jusef asked a simple question, "Are we free to move about?"

"Where do you wish to go? What would you do? You are in the heart of the enemy camp. This is not a vacation."

Jusef returned a bewildered look.

"You are free to leave, but not without escort. This is not only for your safety but for the safety of everyone."

Lazar outlined his orders: "Someone will instruct you in the use of remote control devices. If you master the lesson, you will be permitted to have some time to yourselves. Today you will be busy. We will work on driving, mapping out the city and vital points of interest to our mission. You will be pleased once you see your quarters for this evening." The house around the corner from their present location was a palace compared to where they stayed the night before.

6 | THE "A" PLAN

NEXT, I WAS TO FIND JUSEF AND FREE HIM FROM ALI'S influence. My plan called for an immediate return to Hamburg by way of the Zagreb Airport. I must have Mayer check with airport security in case they left by plane.

"Good morning, Karl," our phone conversation began.

"Good morning, Thomas. How was your reunion?" Mayer asked.

"Everything started well and turned into a fiasco. I will explain later. Make arrangements for my flight home from Zagreb and meet me at the police office in the main terminal."

He responded, "Certainly. Is there anything else?"

"Bring my laptop and find out if Ali or Jusef's names show up on any departing flights from Zagreb or any other airports."

"See you there," he concluded as I snapped my cell phone shut.

Aunt Katrina smiled at me while pouring a fresh cup of coffee. I thought of apologizing for the last night's events, but knew she already understood. I returned her smile and welcomed the caffeine.

Surprisingly, my assistant was already at the gate along with a Hamburg Airport Police Officer to escort us through security checkpoints. Karl handed me part of the paperwork with the information I requested. Two of my investigators were waiting outside my Audi, parked curbside. Karl was my right hand.

"I thought you might need this." He handed over my gun. The laptop was on the seat.

"Karl, I do not know what I would do without you," I commented as we drove away.

I perused the information that he provided on short notice. Ali's name was circled, but Jusef was not on the list. I continued to scan the folders. An accompanying memo indicated there would be more information later.

"Remember to check with MEK for current investigations at the Technical University."

"I will contact them as soon as we return."

We arrived in front of Ali's building: a red brick four-story apartment typical for the neighborhood, except this one had every shade drawn. We walked past an arch with the Star of David woven on an iron gate attached to the side of the building, the remains of a synagogue destroyed by Nazis in 1938. Following the war, this very spot was converted into an apartment that today houses Islamic students.

In an attempt to find someone residing in Unit 3-C, we looked for anything out of the ordinary. Slowly moving down the vacant hallway listening for sounds from any of the inhabitants, we came to Ali's unit. The door was locked. A faint odor of disinfectant seeped from the room. Knocking and waiting for thirty seconds, no one answered.

"Karl, get the manager to let us in. Have the other guys check the trash bin."

On Karl's return, the olive skinned manager could have been in his twenties. With a full beard, his age was difficult to determine. I asked, "Do you know who lives here?"

"That apartment has been empty for quite some time."

The sterile smell of disinfectant was stronger as I neared him. The fumes were coming from his clothing and hair. "Were you cleaning something today?"

"No, I was not."

"When was the last time someone was in there, including you?"

"I told you; not for some time. No one has been in there."

"Open the door!"

The door swung open, revealing the air throughout the premises reeked of chemicals. Karl went over to both windows and threw open the sashes. Fresh air gushed in, providing some relief. "Do you want to continue this game?" He hung his head in defeat.

"Give me your identification papers!" He fumbled through his wallet. He brought out a student identification card. The photo did not look like him.

My two officers had completed a thorough search of the trash and basement storage areas. They turned up nothing. I instructed them to watch the area and stop anyone who leaves.

Stepping back into the hallway, two MEK investigators were standing outside and listening. "We are here to check this out. What sort of investigation are you conducting?"

Pointing to the young manager, I stated, "This man is hiding something. Here is his identification."

The MEK supervisor turned to look over the manager's identification, and smiled, "Who provided you with this?"

He continued staring at the floor, refusing to answer. "How much did you pay? Who are your accomplices? How long have you been in Germany?" He remained silent.

"Thomas, what are you doing here?" one of the investigators asked.

"My nephew is missing. The man who was living in 3C may know where he is," I pointed to the empty unit. "I came here to check for him."

"Does your nephew live here?" the investigator asked.

"No, but his friend Ali does."

"Ali who?" the investigator asked.

"I think Amman was his last name, but I am not sure. I only met him a couple of times. I am worried about my nephew, Jusef Al' Obaid. He may have gotten himself involved with this group."

"Do you have a photograph of your nephew?"

"Not with me."

"Is your nephew a German citizen?"

"Of course, he is my sister's son, born in Cologne. His father was from Baghdad. But, his friend Ali is an Iraqi national."

"This is very interesting, Thomas. We would like a photo of your nephew and Ali so we can help you find them," the investigator said.

"I only have a photo of my nephew. I can bring a copy to your office."

"No need; we may have a photo of both of them in our files." His words confirmed my suspicions.

The other investigator handed his cell phone to me, "This call is for you—"

MEK head Gus Petersen spoke, "What are you doing at this apartment in the Harburg district? We need to talk—"

"When?"

"Now!"

"Where?"

"Headquarters."

"Okay, I will be there in a few minutes."

I turned back to Karl, "I do not trust this Ali. I believe he has involved my nephew in some sort of conspiracy plot."

Gus Petersen, with whom I had been familiar, answered my knock. He handed me seven photos and I went through them. "Take a look at these. Do you recognize any of them?"

I said, "This is my nephew, Jusef, and this one is Ali. The others I have never seen before."

"Those are not the names we have," Petersen said, as he laid another array of photos of Jusef and Ali on the desk. "The surveillance photos were taken by us at Hamburg Technical School, their Mosque, and in front of Café Arabesque in Istria. Here are the latest ones from Zagreb Airport with assistance from Croatian Security."

Staring at the glossy photos of Jusef and Ali, I asked, "What names are they using?"

"Joseph Müeller and Ali E'Bay."

"Joseph Müeller is my uncle's name! Now he is dragging my family into this. We must find them as soon as possible."

Confidently, Petersen said, "Ali E'Bay and Joseph Müeller are in Canada with their fake passports; the other five are in Mexico as of two days ago."

"Where in Canada?"

"Montreal, Quebec," he replied. "We must turn this over to the RCMP, Mexican authorities, and the FBI," I insisted.

He informed, "We have already done so."

"What do you recommend?"

"Right now, nothing, unless you know their destination or who sent for them."

"There was an email from a mosque in Baghdad before they came to Germany. My other nephew may still have the email address on his computer."

I used the stairs to rush to my office and located the note to check on the email address. This facet was not a priority until now with all that had happened. Hopefully, Gabriel still had the message.

"Hello?" my sister answered my call.

"Sunny, would you please forward to me that email Gabriel received from Jusef? Remember, the last one he sent from Iraq prior to leaving."

"Sorry, that was a while ago. I am sure he deleted the message. Why must you have this email?"

"The information could be very important. Would you please try to find this email?"

"Gabriel is on the computer now. Shall we have a look and call you back?"

"No. I can remain on the line."

Minutes later, she informed, "Sorry, the message was deleted, but Gabriel says the address was automatically added to our computer address book. The Internet Service Provider was AcmeInc.com. Have you heard anything more?"

"Yes. He left Croatia with Ali, and this address may help me locate them."

"I am worried. Where are they?"

"This too worries me. I am not certain where they are, but I will notify you if we find something more on this. Please call me at once if you hear anything from Kristina."

"Do you think they went back to Baghdad?"

"Not likely, but I will check."

"Thanks, Tommy. Call me later if you need something."

"Alright, talk to you soon."

Upon returning, Mayer was still working on the flight lists with the others. Handing Petersen the note, I told everyone, "The original message was deleted but the ISP from Baghdad was AcmeInc.com."

He went to another computer and typed in *Acme, Inc.*, asking, "Where they are they located?"

A brown, green and blue world map popped up on the ten-foot screen, yellow dots in black circles showing locations of major cities. We saw blinking red lights identifying the locations of Acme, Inc. terminals all over the world. New York, Los Angeles, London, Paris, Tokyo, Teheran, Toronto, Montreal, Berlin, and Hamburg began lighting up on the map. Petersen commented, "This appears to be an active network. We must find out who they are and what they are doing," as he changed the computer query to *ongoing investigations*. Hundreds of case files came up.

Surprised, I heard, "hmmm" slip from his throat.

"They appear to be very well organized. Can you tell which messages were sent on a specific date?" I asked.

"Of course, but our officers have only located the terminal in the host city, not the physical addresses."

He discovered the times of every message that was sent from the Baghdad network on that date. Systematically entering Sonja's address, he brought up her messages for that day. The time and Internet address of the mosque email matched Sonja's inbox exactly.

"The next two messages originating from Acme, Inc. were sent simultaneously to Hamburg and Cleveland. This shall take some time, but we may be able to retrieve some content from these messages, if not all," Petersen said.

"You have found my Cleveland connection," I concluded.

7 | AMERICANS AND THE DESERT

LYING AWAKE ON THE BED WAS USELESS. ANOTHER NIGHT brought more pacing across the room from the door to the window and back. Peering out for the hundredth time at the exact night scene, I grew weary of the same view. I slumped into the floral chair, propped my feet up on the bed and stared at Gabriel, who had drifted off to sleep several hours earlier.

Anxiety over Jusef had become an obsession that filled quiet evening moments, turning me into a full-fledged insomniac—not to mention my innermost fear for Kristina's safety. My memories of Somalia during military service conjured up nightmares of what she was experiencing at this moment in Baghdad. How was she coping day to day? Did she sacrifice food and shelter, and above all—was she safe? A sudden urge to place a call came over me. A glance at my watch indicated that in Baghdad the time was approaching midday.

"Hello, Kristina?"

"Thomas?" she cried. "I am so glad to hear your voice. Our power and communications have been out until today. Yours is the first call we received in the last few days. The ring startled us, but we are happy you called."

"How are you surviving?"

"We are well, but keep a low profile. Assam has been conscripted to assist the Americans in their search for radioactive materials. Naturally, they will not permit him to leave. We are both uncomfortable living under this foreign occupation."

"You should have come home with Jusef. I can still help you leave."

"I cannot leave Assam after he was good enough to come here to help me. Besides, Jusef is safe with you."

I began to imagine her struggle as flashbacks from my police service in Afghanistan came to mind. *Was she concealing western features beneath her burka? Were they close to a combat zone? Do they have decent food?* "What has been happening there?"

"When we are not taking cover from explosions, I see the pitiful faces of women waiting to learn the fate of their men. We cannot escape the whaling and lamentations for the dead."

"The biggest tragedy of war is that innocents always suffer. I need to expedite Assam's release. Is there anything I can do to help you from here?"

"Nothing. The new government here is like the electricity: our situation changes from day to day. I am worried—yesterday, Security took Assam in for questioning for the third time. The same interrogators accused Mohammed of associating with a group of ex-army officers connected to the insurgents. They call everyone a collaborator, but they have no evidence, only the fact he is Mohammed's brother. Assam thinks his interrogators were CIA."

"Have our diplomats provided any assistance?"

"They tell us to be patient; they are working on our case."

"What do you mean *our case*?" I wondered aloud.

"I fear they are suspicious of me as well."

"That is ridiculous. You have done nothing suspicious— have you?"

"Of course not."

"Thank God. I will re-contact my diplomatic connections right away."

She changed the subject, "You have not mentioned Jusef. How is he?"

I delicately worded my response. "I have some concerns. He and his friend, Ali, seem to have taken off on an unknown adventure. Did he say anything to you about leaving or where he might go?"

"They are missing? He was supposed to be safe with you in Germany!"

Following a silent pause, I pled my case. "Sometime during our reunion, Ali left and apparently took your son with him. We searched the farm and surrounding area unsuccessfully. Consequently, I returned to Hamburg the next day, and checked the student apartments in Harburg and found Ali had moved out. That is when I learned from Sonja that Jusef did not return to her home either." My sister's weeping voice pierced my heart. A new dilemma: Should I remain silent or reveal everything?

"Kristina, I have ordered our police to find them. We are doing everything possible."

"Promise you will call me when you know something, anything."

"I promise."

Silence, then dial tone signaled the connection was lost. Did she hear me? After trying to re-connect, the overseas operator stated there was unknown trouble on the other end.

Assam burst into the apartment, breathless after racing up four flights of stairs, exclaiming, "We have been granted permission to enter the Green Zone." Seeing Kristina holding the telephone, he asked, "Have there been any calls?"

"Yes, one call, but the phone is out of commission again. Thomas asked how we are getting along and offered words of encouragement. Hearing his voice was so nice." Tears fell from her eyes and began streaming down her face. She did not share Assam's enthusiasm. "Jusef is missing. I must return to Germany.

We should not have to wait three days to obtain permission to visit a government official for exit visas." She returned the phone to its plastic holder.

"I agree with you one hundred percent, but we must go now. I drove past the international area and there were only 50 or 60 vehicles waiting in line at the first checkpoint. Besides, the temperature now is cool at 31C this morning. I am worried the VW will overheat in the afternoon sun."

She followed him down the stairs, adding in jest, "If enough people run out of gas, possibly the line will be gone in a day or two."

A refreshing breeze rushed into the car on the 15-minute ride to their first obstacle. Iraqi Police and American soldiers manned a checkpoint where a barricade of sandbags and several military vehicles funneled the traffic into a single lane for inspection. One Iraqi policeman and an American soldier approached Assam and demanded an explanation of his business inside the safety zone. Assam presented the permission slip. As they checked the paperwork and identification, the other members of the detail performed a vehicle inspection. The men slid mirrors under the car to look for explosives, and examined every conceivable hiding place while searching Kristina's car. They both nodded, then signaled Assam the car was approved, and to advance to the next checkpoint.

American soldiers wearing dark sunglasses approached their car from behind the second checkpoint. Reinforced concrete barricades and sandbags were piled on both sides of the road. Two soldiers manned a machinegun mounted behind the sandbag wall. Assam and Kristina tried to look at several of the soldiers' eyes, but each one wore the same coal black sunglasses similar to the security at the first roadblock. The soldiers subjected both of them to the same routine questions as to the visitors' purpose for entering the walled city. The redundant questions along with an attitude of superiority transmitted an underlying message that people wishing to enter the *Emerald City* did not belong inside these fortress walls. To Assam, the conquerors obviously feared their subjects. Thirty to forty minutes later, they passed through the second checkpoint.

On their third stop, corporate mercenary operatives detained Assam and Kristina or as the media referred to their protectors: *private security forces.* Assam considered this group the most dangerous. Security forces answered to no one after grants of total immunity by the U.S. and Iraq's new government. He believed this private security group topped the previous ones as a final test for anyone wanting to enter the world's newest democracy kept hidden from its citizens in this military compound.

Kristina found the uniform black lenses on each of the security forces commonplace, and a bit comical. She proposed in German, "We must buy a pair of these sunglasses once we are inside."

Assam smiled and countered, "The government may issue them once we pass their tests." They both broke into subdued laughter.

"English, speak English. We do not understand you. You will not be permitted to enter," the guard ordered.

Within seconds of hearing the guards' raised voices, two armed men stepped out from the metal shack, weapons at ready, while several others peered out from behind tinted windows. The only sound came from a running air conditioner protruding from the side window of the security hut.

Assam reached out his hand, holding their papers, causing the muscular guard to bark out a command, "Freeze! Don't move; keep your hands inside the vehicle; remain perfectly still until I tell you to move." Assam and Kristina nodded in compliance.

Following their brief armed encounter, a man in charge peered inside the car, now turning into an oven. He ordered the blue-eyed woman with the Arab driver to remove her headscarf. Two additional troops behind the sandbagged wall were signaled to step forward and assist in the search. Another came out of the office and replaced the two behind the 50 caliber machine gun.

The man in charge signaled the reinforcements to open both doors.

"Step out of the car." He pointed with his pistol to a spot about 10 meters away. "Stand over there."

Their interrogator turned routine questions into accusations as to their purpose, while the others began a new investigation. The fishing expedition started with Assam. The wave of an electronic wand was followed with a pat down.

When they turned to Kristina, Assam protested, "Leave her alone. She has done nothing."

"Keep Quiet!" one of them shouted from behind.

She spoke calmly, "I am okay. They are just doing their job."

Under the scorching desert sun, the usual thirty minutes of questioning and examining documents dragged well past an hour. The interrogator reacted disapprovingly to their relationship with Mohammed. As the security men scurried back into their air conditioning, the main man granted them entry into the *Forbidden City*.

"You may pass. By the way, where does your brother, the policeman work?"

Puzzled, she hesitated, then responded, "In Hamburg."

Driving away, Assam sighed, "I never thought I would miss Saddam's Republican Guards and secret police, but these Hollywood soldiers appear to be much worse."

A four-in-the-morning documentary about Iraq on a Cleveland TV station brought me back to the present. The narrator exclaimed *United States' Armed Forces are the greatest military ever manufactured. Technically excellent, superior to any force invented to date, capable of changing everything short of the weather, terrain or urban warfare surprise attack, their mission is to rid the world of terrorism. Until this war, terrorism was addressed by law enforcement agencies. Now, offensive style attacks by the insurgents have changed all that. No one will ever forget the loss of thousands of Innocent Americans on that day: Nine-Eleven.*

An American general being interviewed gave a stern warning: *Get ready, because we don't play 'hide and seek' with our attackers. We come prepared to take on any resistance. On the sea, in the air or in and under the land, our troops will capture the enemy. Our military defends the United States of America and democracy at home or around the world. The sea, mountains, jungle, desert or urban centers will not hide the group who sides with terrorists."* His message was clear: I must find Jusef before they do.

A couple hours later, I phoned Mayer to exchange information. I intended to give him a full report on my findings and obtain his updates. MEK still had them in Windsor, and there was nothing new from the FBI. "Karl, I think we are in the right place. They appear to be coming to us."

"Yes, sir."

"There is another important matter for you to handle. Contact the German Embassy and request they look into my sister's case in Baghdad."

"I shall at once."

"Keep in close contact with Petersen. Inform me immediately if anything new develops. Thank you, Karl. You are very thorough."

In an air-conditioned trailer, the government administrator repeated the standard phrase, "State your purpose for coming to Baghdad and why you wish to leave."

"I came to bury my brother and leave. I am asking permission to return home to Germany."

The man glanced at Kristina's blue eyes, but continued speaking to Assam, "Who is this?"

"She is a German citizen, a widow. She was married to my brother."

She spoke with her head down, "I have lived in Baghdad with my husband for several years. He was killed. Now I wish to return to Germany." She revealed as little as possible, hoping to avoid the red flares of suspicion.

Assam and Kristina looked at each other, as the government man shook his head and commented, "Yours is a difficult case. We are familiar with Mohammed Al 'Obaid, but not you, Assam."

"I have lived in Germany since before the Americans came."

"You have turned your back your homeland."

"My home is with my family back in Germany."

After issuing their exit visas, he shoved the paperwork across the desk in disgust, "For some reason unknown to me your case was expedited. Go home."

With the promise of returning home, they emerged from the white numbered trailer that sat in a row along newly paved clean streets, military people and civilians strolling around. Women wore western clothing, with their heads uncovered. Assam and Kristina ignored activities and surroundings and headed back through the Green Zone checkpoints.

8 | OLD FRIENDS

"MR. LAZAR, I HAVE NOT SEEN TATIANA FOR SOME TIME," YASSAR commented.

"She is on a special assignment to keep Huber away from us," Lazar said.

Yassar smiled and suggested, "We must not let this one become bored. She can be mischievous if not attended to."

"You seem to know her well. Remember when she came to us as an outcast, a Christian from a broken family after her father converted to Islam and moved to Michigan. She had no one."

"Yes, I remember."

"Do not worry, Yassar. She is under my control, no matter how she acts."

A gentle knock on the back door interrupted their conversation. Lazar glanced at the monitor and recognized the face at the door. "I know this man. Open the door."

As the bald man in a leather jacket walked in, Yassar looked out, scanned the immediate area, pulled back and quickly closed the door.

"I have come alone to see my old friend."

For the next 10 minutes, they reminisced of old times, especially their fight against the Soviets. "Lizard, you were the best commander we had in Afghanistan."

"We lost many brave men to expel the Russians."

"Only to be replaced by the Americans."

"Our struggle continues."

"Yes, unfortunately; our work is not done. When I learned you were here, I had to visit you. My mission here is accomplished. I must return to Detroit." He embraced his old commander. "I will always hold you in the highest esteem. May Allah guide your steps."

That afternoon, I phoned Gabriel at University Circle to ask, "Have you found anything?"

"I need more time."

"You have two hours. Meet us at the hotel coffee shop."

"I understand."

Gabriel replaced the cell phone in his coat pocket, and continued walking toward Twing Hall, which was strategically located near the center of Case University. He perceived that Arabs seemed to be everywhere throughout the campus, concluding that this would be just the type of place his cousin could hide in plain sight. The multicultural mixture of young students and international visitors provided ideal cover. He harbored the thought that with a grain of luck he would locate Jusef before the FBI found him by accident. As attractive female students passed, Gabriel mentally noted, *No wonder my cousin chose this place.*

Gabriel entered the campus coffee shop for a cup of herbal tea. He found a vantage seat near the window to observe the ebb and flow of foot traffic for signs of Jusef. While sipping the tea, he casually glanced over his shoulder, aware of four young Arab males seated in the far corner. They appeared to be in their mid-twenties. One of them began staring back. His fixation made Gabriel uncomfortable. The individual who had locked his eyes on him leaned toward the man to his left and appeared to whisper something. At that moment, he felt as if he had seen these men before, but could not pinpoint a time or place. Moments later, the man stood up and headed in Gabriel's direction. Gabriel could feel his heart racing and his hands perspiring as the stranger neared. The man reached the table and stopped.

"Why not join us at our table?" the stranger invited in Arabic.

"Excuse me?" Gabriel responded in English.

The man briefly returned a puzzled look before continuing in Arabic, "How long since the days of our training, brother? Was your trip okay?"

"Do we know each other?"

The stranger switched to English, "I am sorry, but you look like someone we know. A thousand pardons."

The Arab stranger withdrew and returned to his friends. He informed the others of their mistake. As if acting on a prearranged signal, they collectively picked up their coffees and abruptly departed. Gabriel cautiously counted to ten before proceeding to the other side of the café. He wanted to see what direction the foursome was headed, but they had already blended into the campus crowd.

Suddenly, Gabriel felt angry with himself as he realized he might have made a serious mistake. Fear had distracted him from his mission. In a moment, the clarity of what had just transpired came over him. These were four of the seven terrorists in his uncle's surveillance photos. Now he had something to report.

We entered Cleveland Police Headquarters through an underground garage and rode an elevator to the seventh floor. A male detective behind the counter waved at Jay and buzzed us in to the *Scientific Investigations Unit*. We went to a section of the police building filled with record files.

Jay escorted me to a rectangular room equipped with more than a dozen workstations. Several investigators were entering data. The squad room had windows on two outside walls and the inside walls were decorated with 8-by-10 mug shots.

Jay addressed the nearest investigator. "Look after my friend Thomas. I need to inspect the evidence from the homicides and check for similarities."

"All catalogued, Sarge," he said with a smile.

"You have an interesting rogues' gallery," I commented.

"That one is Hans Grau," the detective pointed out. "He's one of our more infamous serial killers. He enjoyed torturing his victims, before finishing them off. Most were drug dealers who he ripped off."

A woman with a heavenly body entered the room, ending our conversation. The strawberry blonde with green twinkling eyes rushed to greet me. Her smile sent a tingling sensation through my entire body. She threw her arms around me, manila folders still in hand. After all this time, this woman still has a special effect on me.

"Tommy, how are you? I haven't seen you in quite some time," Officer Mary Alice O'Connor said, planting her lips on my cheek.

"You look great. How have you been?"

"I'm fine, but things are pretty gloomy around here with layoffs."

Her gold Claddagh ring glistened as she stepped back. Its crown pointed outward on her left hand. Someone had made a serious commitment to her. I thought to myself, the commitment should have been mine.

"Well, at least you made detective. What about your horse?"

"You mean my lovely chestnut, Sammy? I still miss her and the mounted unit. Do you remember our beautiful horses? We aren't allowed to ride them any more. The City still owns them and the stables, but now I only go there on my own time to exercise and groom them."

"I am sorry to hear that."

"Jay rescued me from a patrol car and had me assigned here. What brings you to Cleveland, another vacation?"

"All business this time, I am afraid."

"Well, when business is over, maybe we could get together for a drink. I'd like that very much."

"A pleasure to see you again," amused with her new title, I added, "Detective O'Connor."

"Likewise, Inspector Freiderich. You must see me before you leave. There's something I have to show you." As she walked out, everyone in the room studied her figure.

Jay returned to the room saying, "There is a phone call for you in my office."

"Hello?"

"Uncle Thomas, something is wrong; my mother is hysterical; she called me on your mobile. Her voice was trembling. She fears something terrible may have happened to my father and Kristina. My mother was expecting a call, but the line has been dead for several days."

"I talked to her just a couple of days ago and everything was fine." I remembered the abrupt phone disconnection and added, "I will advise Karl to notify someone from the German Embassy check on them. Call your mother back and tell her what we know."

"I will call you back as soon as I talk to her."

Bill walked into Jay's office and commented, "I really don't have anything to report. I just saw Mary walking back to her desk. How do you get any work done around here? Man, I think I'm in love with her; she's prettier every time I see her. One wouldn't know she just had a kid with that figure; I could touch both hands around her waist."

"Her husband is a lucky man to have a beautiful wife and son," I added.

"Actually, she's not married. No one knows who the father is. That's her secret. In my professional opinion, the kid sure looks a lot like you," Jay teased.

Bill chimed in, "I agree with you. Although I've only even seen the pictures a couple hundred times, there is more than a resemblance to Thomas. Where were you Friday night two years ago, or to be more exact twenty-one months ago?"

Seeing they were amusing themselves at my expense, I decided to stick to the facts. "According to my calculations, we were together in New York." I shifted the conversation to my family, "I have just received information. There may be unexpected trouble concerning my sister and brother-in-law in Baghdad. They could be missing."

Bill speculated, "Could this be more than coincidence?"

I answered, "I do not believe in coincidences." Jay nodded in agreement. The three of us arranged to meet for dinner to conduct a brainstorming session.

On my way out, I stopped to say goodbye. "Mary, what did you want to show me?"

She proudly presented a photo of her blonde-haired blue-eyed son, "He's my beautiful boy." I removed my looking glass from my jacket—was I looking at the Friedrich blue eyes? Could he have been conceived that weekend in New York?

Jay poked his head around the corner. "Excuse me; you have a call from Germany on my line."

"Petersen here; Thomas, I have new information about Acme operations. They have been involved with weapons smuggling along with major drug dealing, and most recently, sent frequent Internet messages to the mosque in Hamburg and numerous other locations, including the U.S. and Canada. According to the BKA, the Americans are watching them."

"Thank you. I will call back as soon as I learn more." I replaced the receiver.

Seeing Mary again was a bittersweet moment. My first sighting of this uniformed goddess was as she rode on her chestnut steed in the Cleveland Police Memorial Parade. I felt I should have kept in touch. She has a son that could be mine, and refuses to confirm the father's identity.

"Who is that woman on the horse?" I inquired, noticing her bouncing breasts, accentuated by her hourglass figure.

Jay pointed to the steed with the police officer atop, straw-berry blonde hair protruding from under her duty hat, "You mean Mary Alice?"

"Yes, the female on the horse. She is beautiful. I should only be so lucky to make her acquaintance."

"You want to meet her?"

"Of course I would. Does she know you?" I inquired.

"You are in luck, my friend. I worked with her father, Lieu-tenant O'Connor. I've known her entire family since she was in pigtails." Teasingly, Jay added, "But you may have to get in line."

"Okay, as long as you put me in the front."

"You can meet her later at the club. Everyone will be there after the parade."

Jay held up his hand, "Let me warn you. She's a heartbreaker."

His friendly warning made her sound even more intriguing.

"We should leave now so I can be first in line."

The blonde filtered in to the club with the crowd as Jay ordered a round. Officer Mary O'Connor was now wearing a Kelly green sweater and blue jeans. She was surrounded by a group of male admirers competing for her attention. Two males at the bar waved at her until she acknowledged them. The admirers formed a scrum and cleared a path to her reserved seat.

The club lit up with red and blue flashing lights. One of her bodyguards had activated the lights on a 1988 black and white Ford patrol car that sat along the wall inside the bar. Now I learned how the 'Zone Car Lounge' got its name.

Mary hugged and kissed both men waiting at the bar and sat between them on her reserved barstool. She took one of the two drinks that were waiting and swiveled around to thank her escorts. She began holding court, rewarding each admirer with a pat, a hug, a peck on the cheek, or mussing their hair.

Watching the suitors compete for her attention, I commented, "I never stood a chance."

"Be patient, watch the show," Jay reassured.

In minutes, the princess began scanning the room swiveling right and left, sipping her drink. She continued to search, ignoring the people around her. Her eyes stopped patrolling and focused directly on us. She smiled and waved at Jay from across the bar. She slid off the barstool and headed in our direction.

Jay returned her greeting and commented sarcastically, "She's looking for fresh meat."

"What kind of meat?"

"You pal!" he laughed.

"Hey beautiful, how's my favorite coquette?" Jay asked as she threw her arms around him and kissed his cheek.

"Fine; how is my favorite *dirty old man*?" she asked.

"Hey, watch that—if your father was here, he'd tan your behind."

"Come on, Jay. Let me buy you a drink. Who is this?"

"Mary Alice, this is my good friend Thomas. He's the Superintendent of Detectives at Hamburg PD in Germany."

"Don't be silly; I know Hamburg is in Germany. How are you, Thomas? I'm glad to meet you," extending her hand.

"The pleasure is mine."

"Say that again. I love your accent. The way you talk is so cute." My silence may have prompted her next comment. "I'm not making fun. I really do think you have a cute accent, seriously," she asserted with a heart-melting smile.

"Thank you." I fought the temptation to stare at her ample bosom.

She flipped back her reddish blonde hair, and yelled at the bartenders, "Another round of drinks!" Turning back to me she said, "You're the first German police officer I've ever met."

"You should visit my country. You would like Germany."

She blurted out, "Are you a big shot?"

"No; I am only in charge of what you call a detective section."

"Good. I don't care much for people who think they're more important than they are."

"Believe me, I am not."

As the drinks arrived, Jay asked her, "How's your father doing? I haven't seen him much since he retired."

"You know how he is, you worked for him. He's still trying to pull the reigns in on me."

I interjected, "Isn't that typical of fathers?"

She took a swig of Killian's Red, stating, "You look like you need reining in."

I held up my beer and toasted, "To fathers!"

"I like you," she declared. "How do you know Jay?"

"Thomas is visiting the U.S. He came here for the Police Memorial," Jay added.

"I like the name, Thomas. How long are you here for, Thomas?"

"Tonight is my last night in Cleveland. I am leaving for New York this weekend. I will see a few friends there."

"What a shame. Who are you here with?"

"I came to visit Jay, but I travel alone." In a tactfully sweeping motion, her arm gently brushed Jay aside, as she slid into his spot next to me.

"You poor man!"

Jay spoke up, "Careful, Thomas is my friend."

She purred, "I'll be gentle." We laughed.

Wailing bagpipes signaled the start of the pipe and drums performance upstairs. Their rendition of 'Danny Boy' drew Jay and the others to the hall. Mary and I remained downstairs with two other couples.

"Now we don't need to shout," she said.

"Much better," I agreed. "Do you want to watch the show?"

"I can hear them any time. Besides, my father's in the band."

Jokingly, I said, "Are you worried about him reigning you in?"

She cooed, "Maybe."

I prefer hunting to being hunted. Over drinks and conversation, I fantasized about bringing Mary with me to New York. Our roles increasingly reversed with time and alcohol. I had changed back to the hunter.

Jay returned with the others from the show and ordered a round for us remarking, "You guys missed a good show."

"You know, we should be going. Thomas has to catch a plane in the morning," Jay reminded me, pointing to the wall clock.

I requested one last round, "Shall we drink one for the road? After such a good time, I hate to leave."

"Me, too," she said, peering over her Killian's Red with her emerald eyes. "Thomas and I were just getting acquainted. Besides, that's bar time—my watch shows an extra twenty minutes."

Jokingly, Jay said, "You two should continue this in New York."

"Good idea!" we both replied in unison, laughing at our simultaneous response. Jay threw his hands up in a stopping gesture, "Mary, Thomas is a good friend."

Mary said, "Don't worry. I'll take good care of him."

I reassured Jay, "Thank you for your concern, but I am in good hands." I looked at Mary, "I will make all the arrangements."

Hand in hand, as we walked out of the club, I could barely hear Jay shout, "I think you're both nuts!"

9 | COMMON SECRET

LAZAR PONDERED WHETHER TO REVEAL WHAT HE KNEW ABOUT Osama Bin Laden. His superiors shared the secret with the CIA about Bin Laden's capture. He was one of a select group entrusted with this classified information. The world at large was only guessing his whereabouts, but a privileged few knew the date and location where Bin Laden was taken. His captors remained silent about the kidnapping by CIA operatives who flew him by private jet to an unknown country. *Do my men have a right to know?*

Lazar knew for some time of the *rendition program*[1] and that some Middle East and European countries were secretly participating. The public's only clue of the incident was from President Bush in a speech on 3-13-02, where he indicated Bin Laden's capture was no longer a priority. He wondered how long this secret could be kept.

At this moment, time is on our side. Our operatives successfully continue to infiltrate the U.S. and other targets undetected. Now is the time to launch our offensive: a thousand stones at the Great Satan in retaliation for our martyrs.

---

[1]Operation Rendition is a CIA secret program of internment by kidnapping and conveying suspected terrorists to undisclosed countries without due process to obviate international law.

In reality, the store on East 105 was his center of operations with soldiers sworn to secrecy about its location. Tarik Lazar referred to his command center as a lizard's lair from his time in Afghanistan. In a blighted area of town, the obscure Al Farad's Market was actually a secret command post for terrorist operations. With a constant hub of activity, arrivals of personnel and supplies, this location also acted as a clearinghouse for intelligence gathering and dissemination.

While Gabriel continued to search the campus area, Jay permitted Mary to leave work early in order to drive me to Der Braumeister. The bar-restaurant was a popular watering hole for police, attorneys and political wannabes. Mary thought the Bavarian atmosphere would be welcomed diversion for someone from Germany.

"Bill and I have some work that has to be finished before we can leave. We'll meet you in about an hour," Jay said.

On the drive over, my obsession over Mary's son Michael's blue eyes kept recurring along with our weekend in New York. My question had to be answered. Putting on my charming voice, I asked, "Might I inquire, who is Michael's father?"

"Absolutely not!"

"Now that we have that cleared up; I am truly happy to see you again."

Her answer came with a heart-stealing smile, "I am too; please, don't be upset. I want to keep this a secret."

I fought back the urge to reach over and kiss her, as she turned right onto West 130th Street. "Why aren't you wearing your safety belt?"

"I never wear seatbelts—they are forced on us by an unconstitutional law," she protested.

Tapping her thigh, I said, "Okay, my Irish rebel." My comment brought an approving smile, as she parked behind the bar. We walked to the front entrance, her arm locked around mine.

She chose a booth in the bar instead of a table in the quieter dining room. Racks of antlers on deer heads protruded from the dark knotty pine paneled walls. Two tapped beer kegs were mounted directly behind the bar. A classic wooden bar stretched the entire length of the room on the left. Dozens of forest green barstools were yet unoccupied. Behind the bar, mirrored glass shelves with beer steins and liquor glasses were covered with an array of liquors. On the far wall, a six-foot tall chalkboard listed two numbered columns of fifty imported beers. A brass and white porcelain draft dispenser stood prominently over the center of the bar. The owner's family was displayed in a portrait of traditional alpine dress as they stood watch over the cash register with stern expressions. German folk music from the dining area flowed in but was unable to drown out two television screens with European sports channels.

"I'll have a Killian's Red, and whatever he wants," she ordered.

"A diet coke for me," I said.

"Something's wrong when a good German like you turns down a beer," she mused.

"I must keep a clear head. There are some important matters that I must attend to." I glanced at the beer advertisements decorating the walls. One caught my eye: *Life is too short to drink cheap beer.*

"This sounds serious. Who are you taking to New York this time? Do I know her?"

"Nothing like that—" Her eyes searched mine. I was taken aback, seeing her serious look for the first time. Sipping my coke, I elected not to confide to her why I was here.

"Are you on a secret mission to save the world?"

"I am no crusader, just a man trying to do the right thing."

Bill and Jay wandered in, motioning us to join them. We moved to their table and Bill ordered beer #37 from the waitress. Jay requested a coke and another Killian's for Mary.

"Bill, have you found a Cleveland connection to Jusef and Ali?" I inquired.

"I located five possible individuals connected through businesses, specifically inner-city grocery stores. Each store relies on government assistance to operate. These organizations deal in cash, buy and sell contraband and redeem food stamps for dollars."

Bill's knowledge included how attorneys negotiated plea deals to prevent their clients often referred to as 'helpers' from drawing unwanted media attention. He was aware of the huge profits some of the stores generated and the scope of the network involved. Sharing this additional information was not germane to Thomas' mission. Cleveland Police were aware of the larger network, but lacked the manpower and money for a proper investigation of this organization. These were routinely referred to the feds—they report those dollars funnel to offshore contacts, disguised as legitimate businesses. His police were unable to obtain citizen cooperation including local informants for fear of retaliation.

Bill continued, "I'm familiar with all five players, but for my money, Tarik Lazar is the brains behind this operation. Somehow Lazar has managed to escape justice. Rumor has it, he is an FBI informant, but *the eye* will never admit or deny his status." He lifted his beer and emptied the bottle in one gulp, then ordered another round for everyone at the table. Bill added a shot of CC for himself as the waitress walked away. Although he liked this bar, he informed us that with the slow service, we should have doubled the order.

Bill asked, "Has your police department undergone any drastic changes because of the 'new war on terror'?" I detected some alcohol impairment in his demeanor.

"Speaking generally," I stated, "Everyone has had to adapt to the new threats in one way or another."

He blurted out unexpectedly, "Yeah, everywhere but here. This whole homeland security thing is a joke. They don't care about us; all the money goes to protect the east coast and Washington. Our helicopter is grounded; the police boats are in dry dock, two-hundred-eighty-six laid off. The feds took over our airport and plan to replace us with private security." He rambled on, "I remember when we were a police department—not armed social workers. New officers don't know how to investigate; they just sit in front of computers, I swear they're playing video games." Looking at me, he asked, "Where do they think all that information came from? Somebody has to be on the street to get it; nobody is out there talking to the people. Cops used to know everyone on their beat, and detectives knew the bad guys. The game had rules, favors were exchanged, and there was a constant flow of information. Now they sit in front of computers and fill out forms for the feds. The FBI is no help; they never share anything important. Actually, I think they spy on us. There are few good detectives left; most are just computer operators. Everything today is a disease instead of a crime; there are no longer any drug addicts or drunks—only the chemically challenged." He raised the glass, "To Aldus Huxley and George Orwell," and downed his shot, then chased it with a beer.

Jay interrupted Bill's tirade, "Lazar manages more than 20 stores, none of which are in his name. He has no arrest record in Cleveland or anywhere else—not a damn parking ticket."

Bill fired back, "That's right; and how do you know that? Because you are out there, on the street where you belong."

I joined the toast, "Old school."

Jay's phone rang. "Thomas, I spotted four of the terrorists from your photos," Gabriel shouted.

Jay handed me his phone. "It's for you."

"Calm down. Are you certain?" I asked.

"I am positive. One approached me thinking I was Jusef."

"We must confirm your suspicions with my photo array. Where are you?"

"I am at the University's coffee shop."

"Stay there. We are on our way."

Lazar decided to permit the young recruits to visit the university campus after instructing them to maintain a low profile. Yassar drove Jusef and Ali to University Circle and suggested they stop by the Islamic Book Store. He instructed them to return on the train to East 105ᵗʰ Street.

He frowned and reiterated Lazar's serious warning: "Do not attract attention; stay out of trouble, and most importantly, don't be late!"

They half ran to their destination, excited at their brief release from captivity. Reaching the bookstore in minutes, the door was locked although customers were inside. A button with a sign in English read: *ring doorbell to enter*. Ali pressed the button and a buzzer sounded as the door came free. The two bumped shoulders playfully as they entered.

"They just arrived. I'll call you later," the woman pressing the buzzer said.

Jusef immediately noticed her long black hair, long legs and slender tall figure, speaking on a cell phone. Jusef stole a glance at every opportunity. Trying not to be obvious, the pair went over to a part of the store where Ali picked up an Arabic newspaper and read. Jusef remembered Lazar insisting they keep a low profile, but wanted to speak to the young lady behind the counter. He noticed that she did not look up when Ali was speaking Arabic to him. He started speaking in French to Ali but was not sure if she would respond to their language.

"Parlez vous Francais?" the young woman asked.

"Oui. My name is Jusef and my friend is named Ali," he continued in French.

Tatiana spoke mostly Arabic at home because her grandfather was from Lebanon. She smiled at Jusef, "My name is Tatiana Ali; we have a few books in French if you would like me to show you."

Jusef forgot about his friend and the mission. He was now concentrating on Tatiana Ali. Now close enough to sense her perfume and look at her face, he studied her smile. In his imagination, her beautiful hand reached out to his when she pulled a couple old French Travel Books to the Arabian Peninsula and Africa from the shelf. She tried not to appear so interested in Jusef but she could not help displaying female curiosity why this blue-eyed

Arab-speaking Frenchman was in Cleveland looking at Arabic and African travel books.

Ali grew impatient. He grabbed Jusef's arm, pulling him out of her listening range, whispering in Arabic, "Why did you tell her our names? You are Paul, remember?"

"I forgot. She made me nervous," Jusef whispered back.

"We must go back to the train station, now—before we are in trouble."

Jusef had something else in mind that did not involve his friend. His attention focused on the figure in the tight skirt and fully shaped sweater. Her silhouette distracted him from everything else.

"You go back. I am staying here." Jusef turned away from Ali and shyly approached the female clerk and in a cracked voice invited, "May I ask you to dine with me after you finish work?"

"I will be off soon if you and your friend would like to wait," Tatiana said.

"My friend has a previous engagement," Jusef proposed as he walked back to Ali, who impatiently leafed through a magazine. Jusef shielded his mouth with the magazines, and asked, embarrassed, "Ali my friend, do you mind leaving without me?"

He protested, "I do not like this. This girl is too friendly, she is not normal and you are acting strange."

Jusef impatiently scolded his friend, "She chose me—you are jealous."

"No! We are not here to make friends, or chase women. Something is wrong about her. I have a feeling." With an angry face, Ali looked away.

"That is the way Americans act—very friendly," Jusef smiled.

"How would you know?"

"I do not know, but I intend to find out."

"Be cautious—you may cause us to be killed! We must catch the train."

"Do not be alarmed, I will arrive at the train on time."

Ali stared back at the store as he reluctantly left alone, wandering throughout University Circle, visiting the Art Museum for an hour, the Natural History Museum, and the Auto Museum for another forty-five minutes. He ventured past the Lagoon to the Botanical Gardens, but his patience was wearing thin.

"Let us go to Coventry; I will take you to my favorite restaurant. They serve Arabian cuisine. We will go by bus." The salesgirl's words reverted to English.

Puzzled, he spoke in French, "Please repeat this in French; I do not understand much English." Meanwhile, Jusef was more than pleased. He turned to Tatiana and continued, "I will join my good friend later. We will now discover more about you and I, no?"

"But, of course," she replied. "Please wait here while I arrange to leave work a little early."

"English?" Jusef questioned.

Tatiana apologized in French, "Oh, sorry for speaking so fast; I will only take a minute more."

She approached the assistant manager in the back room, obtained permission and grabbed her things. Tatiana emerged with high-heeled leather boots and matching leather coat. She slipped into the employee restroom. Activating her cell phone, she quickly dialed a number, "I have a big fish on the line; we will need a large net for this one."

When she returned, Jusef said, "I must meet my cousin at the train at exactly eight o'clock. We have three and a half hours until then."

At the sight of an approaching bus, she flung open the front door of the bookstore, shouting as ran out, "That is our bus!" They sprinted to the corner.

"We were lucky to catch this one," she said, placing the fares in the collection box, "The next bus does not come until 4:50. Do not worry. This will be fun. Are you a student?"

Jusef smiled as he entered the bus. "No, we are here on holiday."

"Where are you from?"

"We came from Baghdad, but I have family in Germany and America—and you?"

"I am an American born right here in Cleveland."

"What is your family name? You appear to be Middle Eastern."

"I am called Tatiana Ali. My family came from Lebanon years ago. They wanted to escape the constant fighting."

"This is what my mother had in mind for me. So you understand why I am here."

Popping up from her seat, she pulled the cord to alert the driver. "Here is our stop."

His eyes cautiously took in the unfamiliar surroundings as she skipped down the steps and onto the sidewalk. He stared at her long dark hair and wondered what his new friend had in mind. Mesmerized by her beauty, he ignored her French and followed blindly.

"Come, we are wasting time. Aladdin's Restaurant is just up the street." Waving for him to follow, she waded through the pedestrian traffic.

"This is my favorite hangout—Coventry. I promise you will not forget this place."

He watched for any sign of trouble as she led him through the thriving business district past red brick buildings with green striped canvas awnings on both sides of the street. Music stores, bicycle shops, drug stores, a theater, cafés, restaurants and bars lined the sidewalks. Jusef observed older people dressed in business attire along with young people casually dressed in Levis and costumes. Bewildered, he continued staring at the people strolling past, talking, and laughing. Unbelievably, Coventry was overflowing with people and music, yet no signs of police or soldiers.

"This could be my favorite place, too."

Smiling, she suggested, "I knew you would like Coventry."

Continuing toward Aladdin's, past Thai, Indian, Mexican and Greek restaurants, Jusef stopped in front of the Zanzibar. Inside, several couples were dressed in costumes while playing pool, as others sat talking at the bar. A DJ played booming dance music from a raised platform in a corner across from the bar. They both peered through the window at witches, cats, devils, pirates, and cowboys moving about inside as if looking into an aquarium.

"What are they doing?" he asked.

"Today is Halloween, an unofficial holiday. The tradition was passed down from Old England when pagans made fun of Christian beliefs—today an excuse to act silly and party. Shall we go inside?" she inquired while opening the door.

"Yes!"

Stepping inside, he abruptly lost sight of Tatiana in a human sea of movement. Jusef froze, as a blonde she devil dressed in a tight red satin outfit complete with tale and horns danced around him. His eyes adjusted to the dim light, searching past males and females gyrating to a jungle rhythm. A woman's hand with a firm grasp pulled him through a smokescreen smelling of cigarettes, marijuana and spilled alcohol. Tatiana led him to the safety of two guarded seats.

"Thanks, Mick," she shouted, leaning closer to make herself heard.

The masked man behind the bar acknowledged her with a slight nod. The bartender was wearing a black knit polo shirt that accentuated his well-defined biceps and shoulders. His dark roots showed through blonde hair tied back with a rubber band on his ponytail. His exact age was a mystery, hidden by a turquoise Mardi Gras mask outlined with white seashells and blue peacock feathers.

She held up two fingers to order, as an authoritative voice from behind the mask questioned Jusef, "Are you 21?"

A glint of fear instantly appeared in Jusef's eyes as he stammered, "Uh, err, uhmm."

Tatiana intervened, "Hey, are you starting something new, Mick?"

The masked man poured two glasses of red wine and winked as Jusef smiled back at him. Jusef turned to Tatiana, "I think he likes you!"

She threw her hair back and laughed, "No, he likes you!" Lifting her drink, she toasted, "To a wonderful vacation!"

As quick as the glasses clinked, he downed his. She smiled enticingly, "Another, oui?"

"What kind of wine was that? I do not drink much," he responded.

Tatiana winked at the bartender, "Mick, more wine." Her cell phone went off. Glancing at the caller ID, she muted the phone. "The caller was no one important."

"You must come here often," Jusef speculated.

"I do occasionally on my way home. I live down the street."

"How convenient."

Tapping her glass against his second larger glass, she said, "Cheers!" Sipping her first, Jusef drained his second. "Please, bartender, another for my friend." Mick smiled and poured.

Looking at Jusef, she asked, "Do you dance?"

"Yes, but never like this," pointing to the mixed couples on the dance floor, "not with women."

"Please, save our seats, and watch our drinks; we are going to dance."

Mick gave them the *thumbs up* as she led Jusef to the dance floor. A full-mirrored wall across from the bar projected the illusion of a much larger crowd. She began swaying her round hips, moving up and down with her arms rising with each beat. Her new friend joined her amongst the costumed revelers.

Jusef scanned the room as his body awkwardly moved side to side. His eyes locked onto a cat woman thrusting her hips and tail at him. Tatiana teasingly asked, "Do you see something that you like?"

Jusef stared into her eyes, "You."

Tatiana motioned him closer with a wave of her hand. She embraced him around the waist pulling their bodies together until they were gyrating into each other. Against the backdrop of rock music and clacking cue balls, all of his inhibitions disappeared with the wave of her hand.

She placed his hand on her derriere. "How are you doing?"

He shouted in her ear, "I have never experienced anything like this in my life!"

Tatiana pulled at the neck of her sweater. "I feel warm, how about you?"

"The room is getting a little hot."

A childlike laugh emanated from her mouth as she squeezed his hand and led him back to the bar.

"Would you like more wine? I have a little at my apartment." The mere suggestion sent wild fantasies through Jusef's mind.

At 1935 hours, Ali started back for the train, passing the lifeless bookstore, a solitary light barely illuminating the counter area. Worried, he occupied his thoughts with the token security and easy access to the buildings he had visited. The lone warrior walked swiftly toward the rendezvous, praying that Jusef would already be there.

At 1950 hours, Ali arrived at the deserted train platform, shaking as he entered the café next door, and took a seat. He watched the 8:00 PM train depart the station. Darting from the stool, he anxiously rushed out the door.

Ali's swift legs rapidly carried him back to the bookstore seeking Jusef or that woman along the way. Once at the bookstore, he desperately checked his watch from across the empty street: 2008 hours. The return trip had been a huge mistake not to mention a waste of time.

Ali's hand trembled as he stood waiting for the train, panting and wiping perspiration from his forehead with his leather glove. He had raced back, obedient to Yassar's command not to be late. Imagining the unspoken terrors awaiting anyone that would go against the Lizard's orders, he silently recalled the *or else* warning. Frantically taking one last look before entering the train, the door closed behind him and the car lurched forward. The face on his Swiss watch read *2020 hours*. With Allah's help, he would not be late.

From inside the faded red pizza delivery van, Yassar spoke to his boss, "I knew Ali was a good soldier. We should have watched the blue-eyed one more closely."

Lazar, seated in his leather lounge chair looked up, "Why? Is he not still with the woman? Are you saying something went wrong?"

"I am saying Ali is the true believer and follows all commands. His friend is the questionable one."

"Remember the two R's: religion and revenge? Our soldiers fight for reasons of faith or revenge. Religious zealots are usually the more reliable of the two. The other one appears to be seeking revenge for his father's death. However, I am not positive he has either forgiven his enemies or abandoned his commitment."

Yassar looked upward, eyes closed, "I pray this is not a cause for alarm."

10 | LIZARD'S ROCK

"WE MUST GO TO MY APARTMENT AND GET TO KNOW EACH OTHER better," she said.

Her victim was struck mute, no longer in control.

"Is something wrong?" she asked.

"No, no; I think your apartment is a great idea."

Time to depart the devil's playroom, they decided and left through Zanzibar's back entrance. Waving at Mick and signaling to put the drinks on her tab, Tatiana led her prey like a puppy. He did not notice her hand slip into her purse and switch the phone to vibrate as they walked down Coventry.

"My apartment is only two blocks away."

The cool night air cleared Jusef's slight buzz, adding to his desire for her. They eagerly climbed the stairs to her third floor walkup. Pulling out a key and opening the lock, the wide oak door swung open to a dark apartment. They flung off their coats as she led Jusef by the hand directly to her bedroom, illuminated only by light from a streetlamp. She chased her snarling cat off the king-sized bed. Startled, the young man took the warm place of the cat. Lighting sweet-scented candles, pulling the blinds closed and putting on music that started with a strip tease, she swayed to a dance, unbuttoning her black blouse, showing a bright red push-up bra that exposed an incredible pair of upright nipples. Right then, Jusef swallowed his Adam's apple, bringing a smile to her face. In one easy move, she kicked her boots off and slid her skirt to the floor, revealing her red silk bikinis, causing him to overheat.

She crawled onto the bed next to him and rose up on her knees. She asked, arms outstretched the way a spider does before a strike, "How do you like my play pen?"

"I like very much," he stared, backing up to the head of the bed.

"Then you will really like this," as she began removing his clothing.

They embraced with heated kisses. She pulled off the rest of their clothing except his shirt. Jusef could wait no longer. He pushed her back and climbed on top of her, entering his princess. She aggressively met his thrusts, quickly overpowering him. She rolled her startled partner onto his back, assuming the top position, taking control. In seconds, he let go, exploding prematurely, feeling a strange sense of disappointment at his lack of power to prolong the moment. She rolled off and lay beside him.

"I apologize. I did not expect—"

She silenced him with her fingers across his lips, as she kissed his cheek. Her kisses moved to his chest and started down. When the kisses got beyond the point of no return, he felt new life.

For a brief moment, he considered, *is this a forbidden act?*

She continued her kisses.

His final thought: *I will think about this later.*

He pulled the gold satin sheets over them and climbed on top of his lover. They created their own rhythm, grinding and thrusting away until both of them lay exhausted. Once assured that her lover was asleep, she silently slipped from beneath the covers to report in.

The temperature was dropping outside, causing the apartment radiator to make a clanging noise, interrupting his slumber. Jusef sat up, then sprang to his feet and looked around the room for signs of danger, moving to the door and peering into the other rooms. He sighed in relief, seeing her standing in the kitchen. Clad in an extra large gray CWRU sweatshirt worn as a nightgown, she was making coffee. He smelled the aroma before hearing the percolating sounds. He rubbed his eyes and focused on his watch—7:30 PM; putting his pants on, he slowly walked into the kitchen barechested and wrapped his arms around her from behind.

Observing the kitchen clock, he asked, "What is the time?"

"Eleven-thirty; what time were you supposed to meet your friend?" she calmly asked.

"Eight o'clock; I was supposed to meet him at the train at eight," he shouted; "I must leave."

Still calm, she questioned, "Where did you have to go?"

His mind quickly searched for the right answer. He remembered the street and the oath never to mention the store by name. "East 105th Street and Quincy," he blurted out.

"That is not far from here. I can call my friend."

"No, I must go now!" he said while grabbing his coat and shirt.

"Do not be ridiculous. My friend can be here in a minute." She made a call.

"I'll pick you up in front of the building. We will save time," the friend suggested.

She thanked him. Her friend closed and tossed his phone on the empty passenger seat of his Blue Buick Regal. Patiently watching the second hand sweep away 5 minutes, he put the car in gear. Within 30 seconds, the friend had arrived from Aladdin's Restaurant. Jusef and Tatiana were waiting outside when the four-door Regal appeared.

"Here he is," she announced as the car stopped and they both jumped in the back seat. "I appreciate you helping us," Tatiana said to the driver, "This is my friend Bob." "Bob this is Jusef," she spoke in English.

He responded with his best English, "Glad to meet you—"

"Luckily I have a helpful neighbor," she smiled, as Bob turned to shake his hand.

Jusef replied, "Merci beau coup." The man's prolonged hand-
shake and roving eyes made him uneasy.

Bob asked, "Where is your friend from?"

She answered, "He only speaks a little English. He is visiting
from Lebanon."

"Where to?"

"East 105th and Quincy," she said.

Bob drove back into the inner city. The gay streets of Cleveland Heights faded in the rear window as they descended Mayfield Road Hill past Little Italy's restaurants, pizza shops, boutiques
and bakeries, and a tall red brick church into the University area.
Cleveland's *green zone* consisted of University Hospital, world famous Cleveland Clinic and Case University campus. Each institu-
tion had its own private police force.

As they left the edge of University Circle, the scenery turned
to buildings in disrepair, neglect and destruction. The streetlights
brightened, exposing boarded up storefronts, abandoned buildings with broken windows, missing doors, and countless pieces
of broken glass sparkling like fresh fallen snow under sodium
vapor lights.

Jusef had barely paid any attention to the driver until his pierc-
ing glances, reflected in the rear view mirror, became more of a
stare. His bespeckled eyes were intimidating, but not frightening.
Somehow, the eyes were oddly familiar. He searched his memory to
make a connection. This is one of my uncle's silent interrogations:
police eyes! This man is from the secret police. I must break free.

After 15 minutes they had reached the deserted train platform. Jusef kept nervously looking for an opportunity to escape.
Tatiana broke the silence.

"I have a French book you might like at the store."

He deeply regretted accepting a ride from her friend. Jusef showed
concern with Bob and Tatiana's obsession with where he was going.
He stared out the window at Al Farad's Store, but said nothing. They
continued several blocks past to another store, Mike's Deli.

"Stop the car! Here is the store," Jusef bellowed in French.

Tatiana informed Bob, "He wants out." He ignored her and continued driving.

Bob said, "I don't feel right; tell Jusef this is a high crime area and I don't want to see anything happen to him."

"Let me out," he growled in English.

"Êtes-vous sûr? Cet endroit est peu sûr," she warned.

He replied, "Au revoir."

She touched his left hand, slipping a small piece of paper inside. He surreptitiously put the note into his pocket, making sure the driver did not see. Bob was preoccupied with a malfunctioning traffic light they were rapidly approaching. As the vehicle slowed to a near stop, Jusef suddenly jerked the door handle with his right hand and bolted from the vehicle. She called out after him, "Appele moi…"

In seconds, he disappeared down a side street. The lone runner sprinted past dimly lit homes, abruptly turning into a driveway between two darkened houses. Entering the shadows, he thought *far enough*, having situated himself at least eight or ten homes away from the corner. Looking back toward East 105, no one appeared to be tracking him. The blue car was gone. I am free.

The desire to rush back to Ali was contained by the fear that Bob may still be in the area. Jusef thought, *I must wait a while longer*. Frustrated with his broken watch, he counted 300 seconds before emerging from the shadows.

Walking back to East 105, he kept close to the brick wall as he constantly surveyed the area. Seeing no trace of the vehicle, he emerged onto the street. He dashed across and abruptly turned left, walking on the opposite sidewalk. Like a shadow, he clung closely to the buildings, trying to stay out of the light. Cautiously passing Al Farad's again, he stopped at the corner. On the lookout for Bob's car, his back pressed against the cool damp wall. Seeing the entire area was quite desolate reassured him of his safety for the moment.

Crisscrossing 105, racing down a side street, he darted into the first yard, running for and scaling the back fence. Landing cat-like on all fours, he remained in position and looked around to see if anyone followed him. He continued his escape through the adjoining yard and climbed over another fence, constantly on the alert for danger. *Almost there, soon I will be safe*, he thought, leaping over the last chain link hurdle. A blinding burst of light struck him without warning. He dove to the ground and lay prone using both hands to shield his eyes.

The silent but effective motion detector caught him off guard. The sensors automatically activated several floodlights attached to the rear of Al Farad's. As Jusef's sight began returning to normal, he observed the silhouette of a man in an upstairs window of the house behind him.

Startled and bewildered, he frantically tried to regain some composure. Instantly reassessing the situation, he crawled toward the back door. One barking dog from a distant yard set off a chain reaction of yapping canines. The howling began to alert the neighborhood of his presence. Lights flicked on inside some of the houses; time to act before someone discovers him.

He continued to inch toward the objective on his belly. The lights went out and the area again shrouded itself in darkness. *A timer*, he thought. He had triggered a timer. *How much longer before the entire area lights up again?* Springing to a crouch, he dashed to the door and searched for a way to gain entry. Desperate fingers located a button along side the doorjamb. One press had instantly activated another light, revealing a camera lens above the door focused on him. In seconds, a hum of electrical current signaled the door was being unlocked.

"Come in quickly," Yassar's deep voice beckoned in Arabic.

Although frightened as he recalled Mr. Lazar's warning, Jusef rushed into the back room without hesitation. Yassar immediately secured the door by placing a board between two metal brackets bolted into the wall. Ali sat erect in the corner near a worn butcher-block table. He did not speak a word or acknowledge

Jusef. His full attention was concentrated on the solitary window in the room boarded up and painted black.

Lizard's hidden electronic eye was buried behind stacked cases of beer and soda pop along the wall. Yassar returned to a folding chair and watched a monitor that depicted an empty and darkened back yard. Yassar hoped that no one had tailed Jusef. When his cell phone rang, Yassar spoke in a whisper and hung up. He left the room after ordering the two to remain silent and in their places.

Lazar sat in his office watching Jusef and Ali with Yassar standing behind him. Jusef waited several minutes before speaking. "I am truly sorry. This will never happen again." Ali ignored him and continued to pray, fixated on the secured window.

"Look at me. How can you sit there and pray, not knowing what direction you are facing?"

Ali looked directly at Jusef, demanding, "What happened? Where were you? How could you do this to me? We are in deep trouble."

"My friend, I would never do anything to hurt you or our brothers. My watch stopped," offering his wrist for inspection.

"A friend does not get another friend in trouble. We were together and will suffer the same fate."

"I will tell them I am to blame."

"No matter; I have been praying to Allah for his mercy all evening. Mr. Lazar is furious with us. I fear for our lives."

"I am truly sorry. Do not be angry with me. This will never happen again."

"You do not understand. This man has killed hundreds of soldiers in Afghanistan and countless others around the world, including some of his own men. He is no one to be trifled with. The Russians placed a bounty on his head, but failed to kill him. His soldiers are masters of concealment and ambush, appearing and disappearing like bolts of lightning. And now he is going to kill us because of a woman."

"How do you know this?" Jusef curtly questioned Ali.

"Yassar—even he fears for our safety." Ali returned to his meditation.

Lazar continued to watch the screens and listen to the two detainees' conversation from his office, better known as *the Lizard's Rock*. Business licenses, permits, and plaques denoting civic contributions to the neighborhood and City covered the walls. The most useful feature hidden under his desk was a secret trap door that provided an escape route through the building next door. Explosive devices concealed along the way would prevent anyone from pursuing.

Lazar appeared in the dimly lit room. He stood over his captives without uttering a word. They looked up into the cold black eyes of a demon.

"Tell me why I should not kill you right now!" he demanded in Arabic pointing a pistol directly at Jusef's head.

Jusef closed his eyes and begged, "I am sorry, please do not kill me! I did not betray you. I met a girl and went to her apartment and we made love. When I saw my watch was broken, I came back immediately. I did not tell her or anyone anything."

He looked up at his executioner when he heard the pistol cock. *I should have stayed with Tatiana. Why did I come back?*

"Please do not kill me! Give me another chance. We have come from half way around the world to help fight our enemies," he begged.

Ali nervously added, "At the mosque, they taught us that *the enemy of my enemy is my friend*. We are your soldiers to command."

They bowed their heads in fear and humility to avoid his cold stare. At that moment, Lazar recalled his brave young warriors in Afghanistan who may have deserved a second chance. He decocked and slid the weapon under his belt.

11 | PERSON OF INTEREST

HOLLYWOOD GOSSIP COLUMNIST WALTER WINCHELL DUBBED THE FBI *G-Men*. From this theatrical perspective, an agency better know as *The Bureau* was born. In 1908, Charles Bonaparte, Attorney General under Teddy Roosevelt, originally created the Bureau of Investigation with 34 detectives and secret servicemen to investigate corruption and federal crimes. During the last one hundred years of foreign and domestic conflicts, the agency gradually garnered increased authority and became the nation's internal spy operation.

Special Agent Robert Huber knew the basic history of the Bureau: That J. Edgar Hoover was the longest serving director, having been appointed in 1919 by the Harding administration. He knew Hoover had a morbid fixation with Munchausen's syndrome[2] as the MO behind why every person reporting a crime to the FBI is considered a person of interest. Rumors as to Hoover's untimely demise grew along with internal politics. Huber found the rumor mill made truth difficult to discern from fiction.

Special Agent Dobbins, who had picked up the seven photos from Thomas the day before, sat at his desk looking over the array. The intensity of his scrutiny captured SA Huber's attention. Huber spotted a familiar individual among the photos and inquired how

---

[2]Condition whereby false victimization is reported for attention or sympathy.

Dobbins had acquired them. Huber immediately recognized the individual he had had in the back seat the previous night.

Upon learning the source of the photos, Huber immediately summoned 'Bugs,' his favorite field technician. He requested his assistance investigating a suspected terrorist cell. The two left in the van for the Holiday Inn Lakeside. On the way, he provided Bugs with his laundry list of things to be ironed out.

Bill called me at my hotel to say he was able to leave work early, but being in charge of the Narcotics Unit, he remained on call. One phone call could instantly mobilize several squads of detectives and a SWAT team if needed. The only call I wanted was from the FBI giving me news about Jusef. Ironically, they were already on the way.

Bill wanted to see if we were ready to be picked up, saying he was leaving from the Justice Center. In a devilish mood, he had used his cell phone from the hotel elevator. The unlikely spy paused in front of our room and put his ear to the door.

Jay swung open the door with a smile as Bill rolled his eyes. "So, when did you get here?"

"Five minutes ago," Bill confessed red-faced.

Jay laughed, "I thought so—I got an A in door knocking class back in academy."

After the four men exchanged greetings, Bill walked into the room and turned up the TV volume saying, "Cover noise; you get paranoid after working narcotics for awhile." Everyone smiled at Bill, who sat down in the easy chair, crossing his legs. "I want you and your nephew to review what you told me and think if there is *anything* you may have left out."

We re-examined every detail to this point, considering the fact that the FBI had sent an agent to pick up the photos, when there was a knock at the door. We all exchanged inquisitive looks, as Gabriel answered the knock.

I asked, "Who is at the door?"

"A man in a black trench coat."

As the door swung open, Bill muttered, "Oh Christ, it's Huber."

Jay announced, "Our Special Agent Robert Huber from the FBI—what are you doing here, Bob?"

"I saw the photos submitted to headquarters by Investigator Freiderich. The SAC upgraded all seven individuals to *persons of interest*. This new status allows us to assist in the search. As of now, Thomas' nephew has not entered the United States officially." Huber's eyes focused on Bill and inquired, "Are drugs involved with this group?"

"No. I'm just one policeman helping out another," shooting back a disapproving glance at Bob.

I shrugged my shoulders and stated, "Agent Huber, we have nothing new to offer. We appreciate the update."

The special agent handed me his card, "Sorry to interrupt; I didn't realize you had company. Please give me a call when you have a chance." He feigned a smile and left the hotel room.

As soon as the door closed, Bill popped up, "That guy is always hanging around our Homicide, Narcotics and Intelligence units looking for information. He has never given us any fresh intelligence or case leads in the years I've known him. This is his motto: *tell us everything you know* and *that's what we already have*. He never adds anything to our investigations. Good luck if he's the one they sent to help you."

"This was my first acquaintance with Huber. An agent named Dobbins took down my information at FBI headquarters and picked up the photos," I said.

Bill speculated, "I think your nephew is here in Cleveland; otherwise Huber wouldn't be nosing around."

I apprehensively pondered aloud, "Why did the agent refer to my nephew as a *person of interest*?"

Bill commented first, "*A person of interest* is a suspect without any constitutional protections at the mercy of the state."

I informed them, "We do not have that type of classification in Germany." I felt awkward here, not able to ask the questions directly and reminded my colleagues of the detectives' cardinal rule: everyone is considered a suspect until the investigator removes the individual from the list.

Bill criticized, "We didn't have *persons of interest* here in Cleveland until the feds and their media friends promoted the words. Now, everyone is using the expression without considering the implications."

I acknowledged, "This is turning into a learning experience for me."

Jay enlightened, "From the photos, the FBI will develop a psychological profile based on each one's physical characteristics. Basically, they have classified all seven as suspects, without evidence of illegal behavior."

Our conversation increased my concern for Jusef. I began to feel helpless in this strange setting of dueling jurisdictions. Who was really in charge and how could they help? Most importantly, what does this mean for my nephew?

Huber left the hotel and walked a half block to his black undercover van. Tapping on the side of the vehicle, the door slid open and he climbed in. Bugs sat on a rolling stool with rubber casters wearing a headset. He monitored listening devices and six nine-inch TV screens.

"How did everything go?" the tech man asked Huber.

Pointing to Jusef's picture, Huber said, "I saw this kid with Tatiana last night. We'd better check the tapes from the pole cameras outside her apartment to see if any of the others might have showed up there," spreading out the seven photos.

The techy suggested, "You might get a promotion out of this."

"Yeah if Popovich doesn't fuck things up!"

"What's he doing nosing around in our case?" Bugs asked.

"That asshole claims to be a friend of the German cop."

"I don't trust that son-of-a-bitch. A lot of cases get screwed up because he's always arresting our informants."

A live satellite feed was broadcasting over a local channel. Four pairs of eyes in room 714 focused on a female news reporter standing in front of a store barricaded with yellow tape behind her. Police officers and a crowd had gathered on the street. *There's been a shooting and armed robbery at an east side store. Yet another Arab owner was killed while defending his store from robbers*, the reporter announced to the viewers.

"Those news jackals are waiting for the coroner to remove the body," Bill sarcastically noted. Since the introduction of live satellite broadcasts in living color, filming the body of a crime scene had become a ritual. One of the technological changes that Bill detested: a curse on modern society viewers came to expect during their dinner hour. Bill continued, "There's no mercy for the deceased's relatives; they get to be victimized at noon, six and eleven PM until a new story breaks."

"How many of these homicides have occurred?" I inquired.

"That's the third one in the last two weeks," he acknowledged.

"Is this unusual for this venue?"

Jay answered, "Yes, all three victims were Arab store owners on the east side of the city. I suspect there is more to this than a simple robbery."

I speculated my thoughts aloud, "Do you think these murders have anything to do with my nephew?"

Bill responded, "I don't know. They could be connected."

A cell phone rang, automatically sending each detective reaching in a quick draw contest.

Bill answered. "Lt. Popovich—Uhuh, uhuh; I see. Yes, I just saw the news. Are you sure? Can you trust her?" We were all listening and watching Bill as he talked and paced around the room. "I would like to meet with her in person; this may be very important, a lot bigger than we know. If she won't meet with me, you will have to handle this; keep me informed. Call me back if she is willing to meet with you. Someone has to interview her ASAP. We must get her statement in writing. I'll be on my cell phone." Bill hung up.

"Was that one of your detectives?" I asked.

"Right; he picked up some information on the three grocery store murders. The wife of one of the victim storeowners says she knows of a group of men from Detroit who approached her husband and demanded money. They threatened him that if they don't get paid every month, there will be consequences," Bill informed us.

"This case clearly sounds like extortion," I suggested.

Bill responded, "Possibly—but she said the husband refused to pay for some kind of tax for the Middle East."

"A tax?" Jay chimed in.

Bill said, "Yeah, some type of war tax."

I was not a bit surprised, but Gabriel's eyes gave a look of confusion. He was trying to follow each conversation in English. The excited tone of Bill's voice told us what he was saying was important.

Jay asked, "Was her husband the one who was killed tonight?"

Bill explained, "No, her husband was the second victim. Apparently the guys from Detroit contacted him again after they killed the first storeowner to see if he got their message. He still refused to pay, ignoring their warning. He was killed three days ago while working at the store. All three victims said they were Americans now and wanted no part of the old world conflicts."

"Do you believe her?" I inquired.

Bill nodded his head affirmatively, and Jay exclaimed, "This is ridiculous; terrorist tax collectors in America?"

Bill looked at his Blackberry and read his colleague's message, "Tonight, the third victim's widow called the wife of the second victim. In her statement she said, *the same gangsters killed my husband. I am afraid for my children. I too am afraid, but Abdullah must be avenged. He was a good man.*"

Bill went on, "I'm surprised she said anything to my guy at all—they are usually a very close knit society. We're going to have to move quickly before she thinks her decision over and changes her mind."

"Or someone changes her mind for her," I said.

"Thank you for your help, Omar. I promise neither your sister nor any of the children will be harmed. I will send my assistant to you." Lazar hung up the phone and summoned Yassar. "Omar needs your help. He is doing an errand for me. Meet him at the West Twenty-Fifth and Detroit store."

"Does this involve the death of his brother-in-law at the store?" Yassar inquired.

"Yes—an unexpected situation has arisen. Omar knows what to do. You are to bring another guest to me. You had better use the ambulance."

Yassar walked to the house across the street, opened the garage door and entered a white windowless utility van. He checked the equipment kept in the cargo area: a pile of extra large and thick black plastic contractor trash bags, duct tape, rope, burlap sacks, chains, concrete blocks, cardboard boxes, blankets, survival knives, machete, baseball bat, axe and a shovel. With his equipment in tact, Yassar drove to the rendezvous. Omar sprinted to the van from his Toyota parked behind the store.

"Give my apology to Mr. Lazar for any inconvenience my sister has caused him. She was emotionally distraught when her husband Ahmed and brother-in-law Abdullah were killed. She wasn't thinking properly when she phoned her police informer friend about the killings. Fortunately, my sister persuaded her friend that my driving her to the police would be safer."

Yassar climbed in back while Omar drove. Yassar crouched down from sight. The van turned into the lot that provided parking for six businesses.

"There she is in front of the drug store, exactly where I told her to wait."

Only four cars sat unoccupied in the parking lot on this overcast Tuesday morning, one owned by the victim. For all purposes, the place was deserted. While Omar scanned the area for observers, Yassar lay prone against the metal wall concealed behind several boxes.

Omar stopped the van in front of the woman and ordered, "Quick, get in." The slender figure dressed in dark clothing climbed in. The van sped out of the lot.

"Thank you for your help—," her sentence broke sharply as Yassar snared her head into a black plastic trash bag. A clamped hand silenced her screams as she struggled to no avail. The unseen kidnapper forced her jerking body into the back behind the seats where she passed out. Once she was gagged and bound, Omar cut ventilation holes into the trash bag allowing her to breathe.

The back door flew open as a November air of reality gushed in on Ali and Jusef. Yassar's figure filled the doorway. He carried a bundle of plastic slung over his left shoulder, motioning them to leave as he passed. They already observed a woman's ankles bound in duct tape protruding from the motionless shroud. The nervous pair saw Yassar descend to the basement of the awaiting Lazar. Omar closed the door behind him and returned to the van. Seeing no one watching, he sped away from Lizard's Rock.

Yassar placed his package on a wooden kitchen chair and cut away the top of the bag, revealing a terrified victim bound and gagged with duct tape, eyes open wide with fear. She offered no resistance to her captors. When freed from the bag, she drew several breaths from her nostrils deep into her lungs.

As Yassar removed the gag, between gasps for air, she screamed, "Help!" pleading, "Let me go!"

Lazar mused, "Go ahead. No one can hear you. You should not have informed the police. You have become a threat to us. We must know everything you told them. Tell us the truth; hold nothing back, and your children will be spared. Cooperate and you will feel no discomfort."

Yassar smiled, nodding in agreement. He abruptly pulled her scarf from her head revealing her long tied up hair. Perspiration along with tears trickled down her face. Drooping eyes signaled her surrender was complete.

Showing acceptance of her fate, she pleaded, "How do I know they will not be harmed?"

"We are not monsters; we are soldiers. Would you like some water?"

Her hands still taped, she shook her head. Yassar held a plastic bottle of water to her parched lips, but she still refused. They listened intently to all she revealed. At the conclusion of the questioning, they were satisfied all was not revealed to the authorities. The Detroit assassins and the efforts to raise funds for the brotherhood were still a secret. This fact allowed Lazar to spare Omar's sister and her family. By contacting the police, this informer had sealed her fate.

Lazar went upstairs and turned up his country music on the radio. His sudden reappearance from the basement startled Ali and Jusef. Their questioning eyes followed his movements until he stopped directly in front of them.

"Is there something on your mind?"

Ali spoke first, "No sir, not a thing."

Jusef swallowed, shaking his head in the negative.

"I have a question for Jusef: What were you doing at the campus coffee shop? Were you to meet someone? Did anyone see you?"

"I was never there," he flatly denied.

"If someone said you were there, would they be lying?"

"I was never there. I was with the girl the whole time. You must believe me."

"Your looks are unmistakable, especially the eyes. If not you, then who was this?"

Oh, no—that must have been Gabriel. He and Uncle Thomas are looking for me. How did they know I came here? Do I tell him? What else does the Lizard know? I must tell the truth; too dangerous for me not to. Will he kill them?

◆ ◆ ◆

Yassar walked over to the side of a wooden landing on the basement steps, pulled away a board from the frame, and reached into a hidden space, retrieving a clear freezer bag containing a white powdery substance along with a brown shaving bag. Returning to the helpless woman in the chair, he placed both items on an end table, and removed a syringe and rubber tube from the works kit in the bag. He used a length of blue tubing to tie off her arm, then poured and mixed the powder with bottled water in a spoon. Applying heat to the bottom of the spoon, the mixture began to cook.

"No, please—my children will be orphans," she begged as he taped her mouth shut. She struggled in a futile attempt to stay alive as her tormentor continued filling the hypodermic with a deadly mixture.

"This will be painless as we promised," he informed.

Plunging the needle into his captive's arm, she recoiled while he injected the fatal dose. Seconds later, her head dropped and body slumped. He waited to confirm the absence of heartbeat or other signs of life. He went about wrapping and sealing the lifeless body in a painter's drop cloth.

Lazar descended the stairs into the chamber of horrors and asked, "How did your assignment go?"

"She struggled at the end. I still prefer the old way: a 9mm to the head instead of a needle."

"Yes, but using a *hot shot* gives the appearance of an accidental death. Think of how many overdoses occur every year."

"True—just the same, I like the old way."

Looking at Yassar, he said, "If these women could have kept their emotions under control and not adopted western ways, this would not have been necessary." The assassin nodded in agreement.

He continued, "The only link to the Detroit connection has been eliminated. The police can investigate all they want, but with her gone and no real facts, their evidence is reduced to rumor or hearsay, no matter how intriguing the case might sound."

Yassar picked up the bottled water, took a sip and questioned, "The usual disposal?"

"Yes, but wait until Simon calls to make sure all the employees have left," Lazar cautioned. "And do not forget to remove your coat. You would not want acid burns on that nice leather jacket."

"Yes sir, I shall contact Acme Plating."

Bill picked up his phone and answered, "This is Lieutenant Popovich."

A narcotics detective reported, "Lieutenant, she never showed up. I'm afraid something has happened to her."

"You may be right. Check around. See what you can find out."

"Will do, L-T."

"I'm watching channel 8. The shooting victim's casket is coming out right now," Bill relayed.

A camera followed the coffin to the hearse while the announcer reported *the victim's wife has mysteriously vanished. Police are investigating. The storeowner's wife is not considered a person of interest; for now, she is just a missing person.*

12 | A PROTESTOR'S OPINION

Reflecting on nearly experiencing death, Jusef vented his frustrations, "I was almost killed tonight, but now feel predestined to fight."

Ali reminded him, "Remember when we protested as teenagers against American Imperialism and Zionism? Are we not still engaged in the same struggle? You, on the other hand, have German relatives who mean more to you than this war. Your newfound relationship with this woman has now confused you more than before. Mr. Lazar will make us heroes and legends back home. We will be more famous than the Sons of Martyrs. Now, where do you stand? Will you go with us or return to your family?"

Jusef covered Ali's mouth with his right hand, "Are you crazy? Never bring them up again unless you want me to be killed!"

Pushing Jusef's hand away from his mouth, Ali protested, "It is not my family who are here looking for me."

Jusef whispered, "Silence," while peering out from their ten by twelve quarters. He detected a foul smoky odor drifting into their space. "The air in this detestable little cell is cold and damp. Are we soldiers or prisoners in this dreary dungeon? I am going to speak out how we have been—"

Jusef's words stopped cold when a shadow appeared unexpectedly. The shadow grew larger and approached. Yassar's presence filled the room, startling both of them and silencing the complainer. He stepped on his cigarette.

Surprisingly, Yassar spoke calmly, "Many times people rely on others to vocalize their opinions for them. Others find complacency and going along easier. But the truly desperate resist in word and deed, no longer fearing the consequences."

Jusef and Ali gazed in astonishment at his words.

He went on, "All revolutionaries face the choice between liberty and death. Each individual must decide for himself."

Yassar walked out, returning to the storeroom, plopping himself on top of a butcher-block table, where he lit another foul smelling cigarette. Strumming his onion-shaped pearl inlaid rosewood oud, his crooked fingers produced a melody of happier times in his life. The soothing music caught the two insurgents off guard.

Ali whispered, trying to convey his concern to Jusef, "I believe you were looking for an excuse to abandon us last night."

"My dear friend, you are my family now. Am I not still with you?" Jusef continued, "I could have walked away and disappeared if I chose. I may not possess your commitment, but I returned, demonstrating my loyalty."

Ali nodded in agreement.

Jusef concluded, "The long hours of darkness here are beginning to depress me. I have never experienced such a dreadful winter."

A dog outside howled at the moon. The bone chilling sound made Jusef shiver as he curled up on one end of the canvas cot. Even the dogs complain in this place.

Ali teased, "Tonight you act like a child crying for his mother rather than a man." He rolled over and feigned sleep. Attempting a positive comment, Ali turned back and suggested, "Let us try to sleep. Tomorrow is another day. We are soldiers."

Rolling back and forth, searching for a comfortable position on the old military cot, Jusef wondered aloud, "How many other restless souls have tossed about on this canvas bed considering their fate?" Jusef conjured up a vision of Tatiana lying next to him with her head nestled in the crook of his arm. Her image and the scent of her perfume overwhelmed his senses as his arms engulfed his pillow, accentuating his longing. He pictured them laying on an isolated sunny beach, with gentle tropical breezes caressing the turquoise water gliding across white sand, erasing any unclean impressions. There, they were together and safe. A shrieking siren outside returned him to his present situation. He mumbled, "I do not care if we ever return home. I only want to see her again while I am still alive."

Ali could not resist one more scolding, "You have defiled yourself by lying with this infidel and denied yourself the sweet pleasure of the virgins in the afterlife."

He scoffed, "My friend, you can have my share of the virgins. I have chosen my woman and her pleasures now."

Ali reiterated, "So be it—but never forget, this is our Hajj and we are the stones thrown at the Great Satan. Our survival is not as important."

With Yassar's strumming in the next room, the street sounds of whaling sirens and horns faded. Jusef rubbed his eyes, as they grew heavier until he fell asleep. In his dreams, he was reunited with Tatiana. Her long raven black hair flowed with her body in slow motion to a fantasy rhythm, beckoning him into the devil's den. Joining the dance, she was erotically moving her limber spine, suggestively grinding her hips and breasts against him.

The pagan beat transformed each movement into a ritualistic ceremony. A mirrored wall reflected the dancers' images as they moved trancelike, souls captured in another dimension, a party from hell with frolicking demons. Right in the midst of the devil worshipers, Jusef's lustful eyes coveted every part of Tatiana. The looking glass reflected the image of masked Mick staring at Jusef's rear end. He sprang up from his bed and began praying to Allah for protection.

Omar took up Yassar's position at the door of Lizard's Rock to cover his post. Omar hoped one day to emulate his mentor. Yassar, now free to dispose of his victim, had made up the ambulance to look like one that was still in service, a feat that Omar felt nothing short of marvelous.

"I will return in the morning," he said, looking down at Omar.

"Going to Acme Plating again, sir?"

"Yes. A necessary evil," he remarked.

The disguised ambulance proceeded west down Cedar with the unlikely cargo and headed toward an obsolete plating business instead of a hospital. He turned left past abandoned storefronts, former banks and dilapidated housing. Another left turn led him past two baseball fields and a couple well-maintained homes that looked out of place. Crossing two sets of railroad tracks, the wagon entered an industrial zone, a reminder of Cleveland's once thriving steel industry. Turning right onto Bessemer Street, the wagon lumbered past piles of bricks and trash, boarded up buildings, warehouses and several abandoned factories. Some businesses had charred faces, a telltale sign of arson. Occasionally, a few scattered lights showed signs of life from some still functioning businesses.

Half way through the industrial ghost town, Yassar turned into a driveway where a building of red brick of the type used in the 1920s stood silently. On the front of the building, a sign read *Ac-e Plat-ng -ompany*. He stopped at the padlocked gate of the chain-linked fence and waved at a dark complected man approaching from the Acme Plating office.

The six-foot-tall stick man named Simon with a black raincoat and hooded sweatshirt stood inside the fence. He acknowledged Yassar with an approving gesture while unlocking the gate, motioning for him to drive into an open overhead door. The stick man ordered an armed guard to lock the gate and close the overhead door behind the ambulance.

Scattered here and there were odd pieces of machinery formerly used in plating car bumpers and other steel products. Yassar surveyed the inside of the building, a few more broken windows repaired than the last time he visited. His ambulance had arrived at its destination.

Yassar cautiously climbed out and stepped directly over to the acid vat. Throwing the switches for the processing to begin, he prepared the equipment while another of the armed guards looked on. A case of mass murder that once baffled Scotland Yard came back to Yassar. He had cautioned himself to leave no traces of blood, remembering that detectives in that case identified the dissolved victims with no more than a drop of matching blood.

Looking in the acid vat, he discovered partial skeletal remains in the process of vaporizing. The questions on Yassar's face were answered on cue when the guard reported, "A couple of local curiosity seekers broke into the warehouse across the street and we had to dispose them."

Yassar nodded in agreement, "I have another one to handle. Call in some of our recruits." He pointed to the sinister black warehouse on the other side of Bessemer, "I will wait here."

The watchman picked up the phone in the office cubicle and called across the street, "send over two of the new soldiers." On hanging up the phone, the guard informed Yassar, "I must let them in the building."

In a few minutes, two Arab men in their early twenties wearing dark hooded sweatshirts emerged from a green steel doorway on the side of the building along with one of the guards. All met at the ambulance, where Yassar ordered the men to remove and carry the wrapped body over to the vat. He walked ten paces before picking up a yellow switchbox hanging from a thick cable that controlled an overhead crane. The machine whirred along an I-beam with a hook and chain attached to a motor suspended from the ceiling.

With a sudden jerk of the motor, the hook swung back and forth along with the chains wrapped around a pulley on top. When the crane stopped over the dead woman, he lowered the chains to the concrete floor. One man wrapped a rope around the corpse several times creating a sling to lift the body. The other man held up the covered torso with a sling hooked to the rope. By pushing another button, the package was lifted to a height of three feet over the acid. Yassar pressed a button that slowly lowered the dead woman's body into the vat to join the digested burglars' remains in a molecular soup.

Proudly, he remarked, "With a little assistance, removing my jacket was not necessary after all." In seconds, the acid burned away the ropes and the crane moved back to its original location. Yassar looked around at the others' ghoulish smiles.

Yassar crossed the street diagonally to an all black corrugated metal building and looked around at the abandoned property. He headed for the side entry door of the fifteen-hundred-foot-long warehouse, passing by three locked overhead doors, remnants of rusted railroad tracks still protruding beneath one of the doors. The quiet structures signaled the area's remoteness.

While padlocking the Acme gate, a guard called out to him, "I will meet you at the warehouse entrance." As Yassar approached, he recognized the black man and followed him inside the property. He waved off the sentries armed with Kalashnikov Rifles.

"We cannot be too careful these days," Simon cautioned.

Yassar peered through smudged office windows out onto the main floor where a solitary figure sat wrapped in a blanket. He huddled next to an electric space heater and watched several television monitors. The hidden cameras followed Yassar's approach from the plating company to the warehouse.

Inside, an overhead crane reminiscent of a giant yellow painted bat slept while hanging from an I-beam track. Several four-wheel drive vehicles, cars, and utility trucks sat parked in three separate rows. Gas heaters hung over a box made of metal framework at the furthest east end of the building, where fluorescent lights illuminated the living quarters of a dozen recruits.

Seeing the stick man had entered, Yassar complained, "The air is cold in here." He could not remember the thin man's assigned name, only his physique. Experience had taught him—better not to know.

He responded with Yassar's assumed name, "Sergey, the temperature is not so much as the dampness from the concrete floor and gaps in the siding." Simon directed his attention to the holes in the wall, partially stuffed with rags and cardboard pieces ducttaped together with insulation scraps. The remaining windows were boarded up and painted over. Apart from a few leaking points of light, the entire building was one giant blackout.

Yassar stopped at a cardboard opening with cold air pouring in, "This may be a large part of the problem."

"Two intruders entered here and met an unexpected surprise," Simon said.

Yassar smirked, "They met our soldiers?"

"What do you think?"

"Where are they now?"

Simon beamed, "They are across the street taking an acid bath."

He commended, "You have made a lot of improvements here. I also notice more equipment and supplies." They walked past rows of unpacked supplies in wooden crates and cardboard boxes.

Simon motioned with his hand, "Come, I want to show you something, Sergey."

The two men headed in the direction of a black box barely visible at the opposite end of the building. Halfway, Yassar stopped at a canvas wall suspended from ceiling beams. Simon pushed back the curtain to reveal several men working. Two were busy placing explosives and blasting caps inside plastic pipes. A third man sealed the ends and stacked the finished product on a cart.

Yassar commented, "You have a efficient operation here."

"Thank you. We still have much to do."

They entered another concealed area where five workers had pieced together a collage of satellite photos to create a wall-sized map on sheets of plywood. The aerial display depicted intended targets. One man marked the map with red numbers, crossing off blue. Another marked black cell phone numbers on pipes. Each of the map sections displayed assigned areas, with one per crew to protect the overall strategy from being captured.

Yassar asked, "What do the colors mean?"

Simon responded, "Blue is for unarmed and red is for armed and ready. The ones we are arming tonight will be installed at targeted locations tomorrow."

Yassar noted the redness of the map, and then complimented, "You have been very busy. Lizard will be pleased."

Simon explained, "We attached the pipes to targeted structures every day for weeks using disguised utility vehicles."

Yassar looked over at the white trucks and vans with ladder racks and pipes on top. He noticed each had a magnetic construction company sign on the door panel. Along side the vehicles, neatly parked rented cherry pickers, equipment platforms and a water truck sat ready to launch. "Considering all your preparations, I cannot wait to see what is inside the black box you wished to show me."

Simon appeared more excited about his black wooden box than the entire plant operation. What could possibly top all that he had seen? Simon inserted the key and removed the padlock to the entrance. Yassar cautiously followed him into the black hole. As the light illuminated the room, he announced, "I had this built for me."

A gas heater was suspended over an open ceiling. The 10-by-12 living quarters had two windows affording a western and eastern view of the front door and soldiers' activities. Brown wooden blinds provided privacy whenever he wanted. The interior walls' bright array of colors provided a warm mix and homey setting. Simon sat on his single bed, head held high. The bright yellow wall and royal blue blanket sharply contrasted his deep black skin.

An orange heavy-duty extension cord ran through the wall to power a 32-inch flat-screened television with a cable connected to the roof satellite dish. A café style chair and table completed the furniture.

Yassar asked, "Are those real?" pointing to a rubber tree plant in one corner and a palm tree in the other, next to a cloth tapestry of an elephant raising his trunk.

"No, I wish they were—they allow me to think of my home."

"I know exactly how you feel."

Simon returned, "I must confess—I miss driving my cab back in the state capital. Remember, I spent several years in Columbus."

"Of course, anything would be better than this dreary place."

"I am not complaining, but back in Somalia, the ocean reaches ninety degrees."

13 | GOT IT!

I WATCHED JAY REVIEW THREE HOMICIDE REPORTS AND MAKE NOTES in the margins as he read. Throughout my career, I look for breaks now and then. Perusing these reports, I recall that some homicides are made to look like robberies. I have an idea. That first store at 89th and Superior was an old convenience store. Do their stores still contain cameras installed from earlier robberies and thefts? I would be willing to bet that one if not all of the stores still use these cameras.

"Are you saying this incident could have been videotaped?" I inquired.

"That's a strong possibility. These cameras don't prevent crime; they only assist in identifying the suspects and possibly provide a false sense of security to the businesses that use them. Just the same, if there were cameras, they might provide us with some vital information in this case," Jay hinted.

After completing his scrutinizing search, I asked if he had discovered any clues.

"I have reviewed and re-reviewed all the reports and evidence. Now comes the time for the ten percent luck factor. We have three chances to find a tape. Can Bill check one of the stores while we check the others, along with your property rooms?"

He called the officer in charge of the central property room, aware that detectives already systematically searched the crime scenes.

"Property room; Johnson—"

"Sergeant Andrewski—"

"What can I do for you, Jay?"

"Has a tape recording been turned in from any of those east side store robbery homicides?"

The officer on duty responded, "No tape recordings were turned in here. Hey Sarge, you could try the fifth and sixth districts property books to see if any evidence was logged in to their property room that hasn't made its way downtown yet."

"Thanks, Lenny. I owe ya."

Jay turned to me, saying, "Tom, every district and every unit has their own property book to maintain a chain of custody. Eventually, everything comes down here for court purposes."

"We have a similar procedure for our chain of evidence."

Next, Jay called Homicide and Special Investigations to see if anyone recovered any cameras or tapes. No luck. He pulled out his phone and left a message for Bill.

In less than a minute, there was a ring in the office. Jay immediately snatched up the phone.

"Bill, could you and Tom go to the stores where the latest robberies took place? You both know what we're looking for."

"Sure, I'll let you know if we find anything. Tell Thomas to meet me out front. We will save time."

I rode the elevator to the main lobby and walked across the plaza to the curb to await Bill. Though impossible, my body temperature seemed to drop several degrees in the couple minutes of standing out in the Great Lakes climate. I raised my collar to shield my face from the wind. At only ten minutes past six, darkness had already set in. Dampness was seeping into my bones, chilling my extremities.

As soon as his car approached, I took refuge and hugged myself to generate a little heat. I folded my hands under my arms and shivered. Bill clicked the fan control to raise the vehicle's temperature.

"The older you get, the more you feel the *Lake Effect*. Welcome to Cleveland," he sarcastically smiled.

"Somehow, this weather reminds me of Hamburg," I noted.

We drove east on Lakeside toward the Arab deli on East 105 and Euclid. Bill abruptly stopped our conversation.

"Listen, did you hear that?"

"No."

Bill reached under the dash for the concealed police radio and retrieved the microphone. "Car 8200, could you repeat that last broadcast?"

"Any car in the area of East 105 and Euclid, assist CFD with traffic at a working fire," the dispatcher responded.

"Do you know what's burning?" Bill asked.

"One of the businesses is on fire."

Bill turned to me, "That could be our store!" He activated the air driven siren concealed under the hood and pushed the accelerator to the floor as we sped away.

"Where are we going?"

"We've gotta find out what's on fire and let Jay know. 8200 to 8710—"

Jay's voice returned, "8710, I heard that last broadcast and I'm responding to the East 79th Street location."

Dispatch informed us, "8200, the deli is on fire at East 105."

Bill acknowledged, "Thanks for the update."

He looked at me and concluded, "We're going to the 79th Street store."

Both detectives raced toward East 79th and Cedar. Bill cut the corner onto Cedar at a high rate of speed. He figured sixty seconds or less to arrive and prepared me, "Be on the lookout, Thomas!"

I yelled, "Look, there! Someone is out front of the store!"

A man was pouring something into the broken front window. Bill cut the headlights and jumped the curb simultaneously. In an instant, he jammed on the brakes as the Crown Victoria slid down the sidewalk. The man turned too late to look up at the approaching car. The gas cans flew off to the side while the man soared in a different direction. As we leaped from the car, Bill pulled out and pointed his gun at a man wearing a leather jacket and hood. The man sprang back to his feet about two yards away. As he jumped up, he pulled a gun from his pocket.

"Gun," Bill yelled to me as he fired *tack, tack* and two bullets hit the man's chest, knocking him back like a pop up target.

I ran to him, kicked away, and retrieved the gun. At the same time, Bill checked the man for another weapon and kept him covered.

Jay arrived at this point with gun in hand, seeing a man down. Bill called out to him to request medical assistance.

Jay radioed in his request, "Get an ambulance! We have a male shot here at East 79th and Cedar."

"How many people were shot?" the dispatcher asked.

I heard Jay and said, "We're okay, but one suspect has been shot in the chest! Notify the shooting team that an officer is involved."

Bill told the moaning suspect, "You'll be alright; an ambulance is on its way." However, the man, appearing not to understand, muttered something unintelligible.

"I think he is speaking Arabic," I said as we knelt over the wounded man. Gently placing my hand on the man's shoulder to reassure we were getting him help, I told him in Arabic to lay still—an ambulance was coming. The groaning young man curled up in a fetal position. My Arabic words seemed to comfort him.

"I knew you would not abandon me, Lizard. Thank you, my friend!" the wounded man said. His statement puzzled me.

He slipped into unconsciousness as the diesel fumed ambulance screeched to a halt. A few minutes later, one of the paramedics said, "We'll do our best to save him but he looks pretty bad. He has a lot of blood loss and extensive internal injuries."

Bill looked at me, amazed at my foreign conversation. "Did you understand what he was saying?"

"Yes. He said something very strange. He called me a lizard, and told me that he knew I would not let him down."

"What did he call you?" Bill repeated.

"A lizard," I said.

The others looked at me.

"Shall I accompany the man in the ambulance in case he wakes up and says something else?" I proposed.

"He doesn't look like he will survive, detective," the same paramedic concluded.

Jay knocked out the loose hanging glass and entered the gas soaked storefront through the broken window saying, "I'm going to check for evidence before the firefighters come and wash down this gasoline."

I stood by with the ambulance with Jay once he unlocked the front door. Bill warned the arriving Crime Scene Investigators, "Sergeant Andrewski is inside. Notify the Arson Investigators this may be connected to the 105th Street Deli."

"Right, LT," the investigator replied.

The storage room was cluttered with boxes piled up on the floor and cartons of cigarettes on shelves. I scanned the shelves on the west wall directly behind the counter area. Using a broom revealed a cable behind some of the cartons. I fished the cable out to look for the end. After standing on some milk crates, I finally found the hidden security camera.

"Jay, I think this is what you were searching for," I pointed out. "As you suggested originally, this antiquated equipment must have come from one of the former stores."

"They were meant to spy on their employees," Jay advised.

"I hope they still work," I said.

I observed Jay push the eject button and out came a tape. My anxiety peaked, hoping that the victim would have captured his killer on tape.

Jay emerged from the front door, smiling with self-satisfaction while holding the videotape, "I GOT IT!"

A patrol car conveyed me back to the hotel following my statement on Bill's shooting. Jay and Bill remained at the Justice Center while I caught a couple hours of sleep after all the excitement. Filling out witness statements will do that to you. I sprung from my feet refreshed and anxious to learn what was on the tapes. A cup of coffee, a quick shower and shave were all that was needed. For Gabriel's protests of hunger and boredom, breakfast and a reconnaissance assignment to the campus area would remedy his needs.

Leaving the warmth and shelter of our hotel exposed us to the tempest outside. The swirling winds' patterns were constantly changing as my emotions were pushing and pulling me in all directions. An urge came over me to bypass the formalities of policing and break down every door until I found Jusef and brought him home.

Gabriel searching alone made more sense. I reminded him of the city's unpublished crime rate. Another youthful face may well blend in among the students. Nonetheless, with unpredictable people, he should take precautions. I instructed *do not act on your own—call me immediately on mobile if you learn anything. I will continue working with my police colleagues. Stay alert. Do not let anything happen to you.*

While he headed to the University, I met with my colleagues. Turning the corner of Lakeside to Ontario, the Orwellian safety structure loomed over Lakeside. Cleveland Police Headquarters was my destination: one square block of glass and concrete facing the shore of Lake Erie and the orange and brown colored football stadium. Continuing my journey on the sidewalk through a sea of people, everyone was scurrying to a warmer place. Entering the main lobby through the one unlocked glass door, a uniformed security guard greeted me. The young officer behind the steel desk was wearing a blue shirt with a round security patch. I was amazed the sentry was unarmed.

"I'll need to see your identification, please."

"Sure."

My police identification and a call to Jay passed me through security. After signing into the visitors' book, he issued me a color-coded pass and gave me directions to the seventh floor and the yellow counter. I was shocked to learn that once past the metal detectors and unarmed security, visitors wandered throughout police headquarters unescorted. A shapely black girl in her mid-twenties directed me from behind the counter to a hallway outside the lab supervisors' offices. Uniformed officers and detectives passed by in a steady stream. Each one carried a file or some piece of evidence with a dangling property tag. Jay emerged from a side door and invited me in.

"Was gibt es neues?" Jay attempted to greet me in German.

"We still have no news in this case," I remarked in despair.

Following Jay into his office, I watched him methodically reviewing the evidence from the shooting. Assured the property was properly logged, Jay slid his bifocals on top of his head and closed the book. He shoved the tape into a video player, and held up his hands, gesturing: "Let's keep our fingers crossed." I helped myself to a cup of coffee displaying crossed fingers and a smile.

"We're in luck. The film is in the right time frame! There's a time and date in the corner." Jay rewound the tape to the date in question. After a few minutes of searching, he said, "Bingo! We have two assassins, not one. Evidently, this confirms the story about the two men from Detroit! I love the quality of this video. Look at the clarity. What a great surveillance tape!"

I commented in disbelief, "Neither man in the video was the arsonist shot by Bill."

After we finished viewing the homicide, he stopped and ejected the tape and put another one in. A few minutes more reviewing, Jay said to his technician, "Give me three copies of each tape, but take extreme care not to destroy the evidence on these. I want stills of the shooters, 8 by 10 shots if you can enlarge them."

"Got it Sarge," the tech reported.

"I've got to complete my reports on what happened tonight," Jay said, "so have some coffee and make yourself at home."

"One question if I may inquire: small businesses in your city appear to be operated by people from the Middle East. Is this correct?" I asked.

"The vast majority of stores are owned and operated by Arabs. They're the newest arrivals and systematically end up in the poorest sections of town. Recently, Indians are buying up neighborhood *mom and pop stores* as we refer to them because they are small and independently owned."

I looked out the window at the City Skyline, "This is the same way in Germany. As each one becomes successful, they leave the poor sections of the city for a better location, being replaced by the next people to arrive."

"Everyone has taken their turn, even our ancestors," Jay noted.

14 | WHOSE DEMOCRACY?

"SEVERAL NEW DEVELOPMENTS IN OUR INVESTIGATION HAVE strengthened my resolve to defend my family, country and democracy," I said.

Jay added, "Right now, we are doing our part to fight terrorism and spread democracy."

The words *spreading democracy* triggered Hans Gruber's comments from back at our family picnic. Uncle Fritz, Gabriel, Uncle Joe, my father, Hans Gruber and I sat at the secluded picnic table, illuminated by flickering lanterns and candles. Aunt Katrina placed a pot of fresh coffee in the middle of our table with a tray of cups.

"Have some coffee, boys. Pick a comfortable spot. No one will be traveling in this fog," she said.

Gabriel posed a question. "What do you think about democracy in the Middle East?"

Hans was the first to speak.

"This new world order is not so new, where one government runs the entire world. We have witnessed this before. As long as good people are lulled by false promises and repeated propaganda, evil regimes will continue to advance their hidden agenda."

"What do you mean?" I asked.

"Evidently, you are too young to remember another European Union. As a boy, I traveled with my mother across Austria-Hungary by train without any national borders," he reminisced.

I responded, "What has this to do with today's Middle East? The coalition forces say they are trying to bring democracy to that area of the world."

Gabriel interrupted, "That is exactly what I said to Jusef, but he asked, 'whose democracy'? Jusef said the Middle East does not want democracy or western ways. He challenged me by asking if I even knew the meaning of the word. He claimed there are two democracies: yours and ours. Yours has free elections but ours are enforced by foreign troops."

My father surprised everyone when he stood up for his grandson, "I believe what you are saying is incorrect. First, do not be so hasty to condemn Jusef. He is confused after suffering a great tragedy, losing his father. He is full of displaced anger and wants to strike out but does not know at who or what."

Uncle Joe stood up and weighed in, displaying his scraped knees and elbows, with disheveled muddy lederhosen, "I tell you, he is a terrorist. He tried to kill me!"

Father said, "Look, everyone has been drinking. This could have been an accident."

Uncle Joe raved on, "Wolfgang, you want to make excuses for your grandson? Okay, but I know the truth about what happened to me."

No one noticed Hans had slipped away until he reappeared from the fog. He emerged holding a full stein of beer. His presence created an unexpected predicament when I noticed a handgun tucked in his belt.

I immediately raised the question, "Who are you going to shoot with that gun?"

"The terrorists attacked my friend Joe. If they dare to return, I will give them a taste of my Walther .380 pistol."

Hans's words signaled Joe to spring up again, displaying his wounds, "Look what that gangster did to me!"

I demanded, "Uncle Joe, sit down. Hans, put your gun away."

"Do not worry! I came to protect all of you," Hans replied.

"Give me that gun!" I ordered. He reluctantly handed over his pistol. "We are attempting to find out what went on here. Please, sit down and drink some coffee." Immediately, I cleared the bullets, making the weapon safe.

"I do not need coffee," Hans rebuffed my offer. He sat down and took a slurp from his ceramic deer head stein. "What the hell is going on here? And why are we sitting here instead of hunting down these terrorists?"

"Jusef and his accomplice will not escape in this fog," Gabriel posed.

I interjected, "Has Jusef actually said anything about terrorism?"

Gabriel pointed to his wounds, "He attacked me like a trained terrorist."

Joe said, "I agree with Gabriel. Jusef assaulted two family members for no reason except to terrorize us."

Hans took another swig, stood up and began, "You want to talk about terrorists? Foreign armies do not bring democracy. I am ashamed for my part in spreading Hitler's new democracy across Europe."

I reminded him, "That was more than half a century ago, Hans. Hitler is dead and no one wants to hear about him."

Staring off into the mountains, Hans flung his arm out, "I remember how the Ukrainians greeted us by throwing flowers at our tanks until they found out our real purpose—and then they threw bombs."

I reiterated, "We do not want to hear any more of this talk."

Joe exploded, "Knock off the official interrogation, Thomas! We can say anything we want at this table."

Reassured, Hans took a deep breath and started again, "To quote Hitler, *Either the world will be ruled according to the ideals of our modern democracy or the world will be dominated according to the natural law of force. In the latter case, the people of brute force will be victorious.*"[3]

---

[3] *The Great Thoughts* by George Seldes (1985).

Uncle Joe pounded his fist on the table, "You are right. They tricked us. We did not know what those madmen were doing. Not only Hitler; all the Nazis operated in secret."

Stepping between Hans and Joe, I tried to calm them down. "That was not your fault. How could you have known? No one condemns you for the past."

"Not so!" Joe added, "Every day, we Germans are unjustly held up as an evil example somewhere in the world."

Uncle Fritz popped up to everyone's surprise with his wisdom: "The death of democracy begins when a country deploys its first domestic secret agent."

I looked over at their faces for any reaction to this strong statement, but I could not figure why they were speechless. For whatever reason, my investigation was temporarily derailed.

The past several days of isolation and incessant boredom were draining Jusef's spirit and dragging him into a depression. His mood alternated between eerie silence and argumentative challenges. With each restless hour, he conjured up a new plan to escape his predicament. None of the American newspapers, books or magazines brought him any relief. They only rekindled thoughts and visions of Tatiana, enflaming his desire to be with her. The fear of Mr. Lazar continued to contain him inside an invisible fence. Seeing the helpless woman taken down into the chamber of horrors increased Lazar's power over him, elevating his level from worry to terror. He prayed to Allah for patience to endure his confinement and the courage and strength to be a good soldier.

The helplessness of the situation turned his desperation into anger that triumphed for the moment over fear. Venturing from the confined area, he cautiously roamed the building, entering an unoccupied room at the end of the paneled hallway. He sat in Lazar's high back leather chair, resting his elbows on the wooden arms, surveying piles of loose paperwork scattered across a battered walnut desk.

A phone sat on the corner of the desk, a lifeline to the outside world. His mind raced as he attempted to remember Tatiana's phone number from the note she slipped to him. Staring at the doorway, he rapidly dialed from memory, praying to hear her voice. Five rings activated a voice message that said she was unavailable. He nervously waited for the tone to leave a message.

"Hello, this is Jusef. I had to call you. I do not know when I will be able to call you again, but I wanted you to know that you are always in my thoughts,"—the machine on the other end cut him off.

Encouraged by the sound of Tatiana's voice, he boldly explored the Lizard's desk. He probed each drawer and sifted through several notebooks whose yellowed pages were penned in Arabic. Struck by the realization that these passages contained Lazar's personal thoughts, he eagerly began to read them.

He continued to examine the papers in hopes of unlocking Lazar's inner being. What was the secret strength that motivated this living legend? *"I am committed along with my soldiers to remove foreign armies that occupy our lands and threaten our way of life. The invaders are spreading their centralized democracy around the world. Some of our people are collaborating with foreign occupiers in return for power and wealth. These betrayers will be dealt with severely. We will fight to the death until every Soviet tank and soldier leaves."*

Nervously flipping through the pages, he began to acquire some insight into this man of mystery who controlled the destiny and lives of so many soldiers: *"With the downfall of the Soviet Union, the United States has become the latest Trojan horse to enforce their counterfeit democracy on the world. I am again committed to take up arms and join the cause to stop foreign invaders and their puppets from ruling over us. We must defeat the great Octopus by destroying one tentacle at a time and removing its eye. Unlike the Soviets, we are waging a war on two fronts. The first is against the American military and the other against the corporate mercenaries that hide behind U.S. troops."*

Lazar returned silently to his office to discover Jusef seated behind his desk pouring over his private journals. Unseen from the doorway, he observed the young intruder. From the corner of his eye, Jusef detected Lazar staring at him and froze.

Calmly Lazar asked, "Have you found any great secrets on your spy mission?"

Jusef was struck dumb, unable to answer.

"What are you looking for?"

"I am trying to learn more about the man who I am serving, a man who holds my life in his hands along with so many others—a man called *King Lizard*."

Lazar returned a twisted smile, recalling the many legends of the *Lizards*. Starting in Africa, during his formal training in Libya, one legend told of a lizard reinvented through plastic surgery. His new identity prevented the Mossad from capturing him in Lebanon. Another version is of many courageous lizards fighting the Russians for years; joining the Afghan Taliban ranks that had direct ties to Osama bin Laden. The newest tale is that of an arms dealer and freedom fighter posing as a merchant continuing his struggle in America. "Do not put too much faith in these wild stories, but look inside yourself for the man who is not afraid to sacrifice for the right to be free."

Jusef posed, "I am honored to serve in your command," thankful that Lazar was not angry at his boldness and curiosity.

"We are constantly looking for men like you to become leaders. We have many soldiers capable of following orders, when what we really need are decisive thinkers who can strategically plan our operations. How much education have you received?"

"Because of the war, I did not quite complete my studies."

Lazar removed a leather-bound book from his library, brushed it off and handed it to Jusef. "Here is some nourishment for your inquisitive mind."

Jusef read the Arabic title, "*The Protocols of the Elders of Zion.*"[4]

Lazar asked, "How many languages do you speak?"

"Arabic, German, French and a little English," he responded.

"You must learn more English. We have great expectations for you. Remember, if you wish to continue in our struggle, there will be no families, friends or comrades other than us. Trust no one outside the brotherhood."

---

[4]First published in Russia, 1903.

15 | STORM WARNING

ACME'S PLANS WERE MOVING ALONG STEADY AND SURE, PRECISELY as scheduled. The recruits complain we are progressing at the pace of a snail. None of them has lost their heads so far, but their silence is disquieting; the time to be wary is at hand. Each phase must come together slowly as in a well-rehearsed symphony with every player performing a perfect solo, culminating in the grand finale. Our intelligence has directed us when and where to move once all is in place. We have detected cracks deep in the defensive armor of the United States. Using a programmed series of events, a staged attack needs to come off without the least hint of our movements until the final hour. To quote the great poet Kahlil Gibran, *we will be like the wind. They will not see us—but they will feel our presence.*

Lazar paced his office as he spoke, "You see, Yassar, while our soldiers are gathering, we are constantly sending misinformation to our enemies, dulling the effectiveness of their security. Color-coded alerts are beginning to lose their credibility with the American people. They no longer pay attention to their government's warnings. Soon they will forget 9-1-1."

Nodding in agreement, Yassar began his report, "Several recruits at our houses are praying more often for strength and success. The blue-eyed one complains that the sunless Ohio weather is unbearable. He constantly inspects the skin on his hands and face. He claims his olive complexion has turned ashen and he is becoming albino. I suspect his spirits are dampening and his will is weakening. He confided that he doubts if he will ever see the sun again rise over his home."

In response, Lazar directed, "Allow the recruits to go outside in pairs to relieve their frustration. They may be missing home, but that could happen to any soldier in a foreign land. Their inactivity is making them lethargic—eyes cast downward, shoulders drooping, and sleeping twenty hours a day. Better to let them out as long as we watch them."

"Late at night, in his quarters, Jusef told me of a recurring dream."

"What was the dream about?"

Yassar explained, "His dead father was trying to send him a message on what Jusef should do. He questions whether he is doing the right thing or merely throwing his life away."

"Why?"

"Jusef said his father was a colonel, the commander of a tank unit that was ordered on a suicide mission to stop U.S. Forces from advancing on Baghdad. Their defense was impossible against the enemy's superior technical weapons, but his father followed orders to the death without question."

"And what did Jusef say to question that he is doing the right thing?"

Yassar continued, "He expressed doubt whether his mission was to avenge his father and countless others like Ali's parents or something yet to be revealed."

"Did he say anything further about his dream?"

"No. I tried to reassure him that he was following the right path by being a good soldier."

That night, Yassar listened in once more as Ali invoked a blessing, "Praise be to Allah for strength."

Jusef turned to his friend, "Ali, what if we do not stay alive?"

"Be strong—we must do our duty, whatever we are asked. If not us, who will carry this out?"

"I have been praying, hoping for a sign. So far, my father keeps reappearing. He walks toward me in an olive garden with hundreds of red flowers sprinkled everywhere, motioning me to him. Then he stops and waits, hands folded, turns and walks up into heaven. What is the message of this dream?"

"I do not interpret dreams, but he seems to be calling you."

The roaring wind and sleet pounded the roof and rattled the windows above the other noises outside the hideout. The sounds from the storm indicated winter arrived early. Jusef crossed Monday November 8 off the wall calendar.

The recruits never fully understood the English of Yassar's radio broadcasting a storm warning and accompanying pressure in the forecast. By now, they trusted the somewhat friendly guard with broken hands. Although he never translated news reports, Ali and Jusef found Yassar's stories entertaining.

One evening he began another tale: "A favorite pastime for us young boys was to gather pieces of rubble from the destroyed homes. We hurled stones at Israeli tanks and soldiers that occupied our neighborhood, then ran for our lives when they came after us. I was up front and did not notice the other boys had withdrawn until several jeeps with soldiers came from behind a tank and surrounded me. I was captured and held down with my outstretched arms crucifix style. They took turns striking each hand with their rifle butts until my fingers were shattered and bloody. One said, 'Now we will know you, little stone thrower, whenever we see you!' I refused to cry, and lay there bleeding as the soldiers drove away. I searched Gaza, but never again saw the faces of the soldiers who crippled me. Individual soldiers are of no consequence. They are all the same to me. But, the day is coming when I shall have my revenge, thanks to Mr. Lazar."

Ali invoked, "We are happy to have been selected by him. Our leader is a true warrior. He has kept us safe and warm in this staging area, and now we are being prepared to strike."

"Why must we wait? Every day we risk discovery. We should strike now," Jusef complained.

"Be patient, the time is not right. Your opportunity to attack will come soon enough. How about a cup of tea?" he asked.

Pondering her lover's fate, Tatiana sat motionless except for gentle strokes on the neck of her faithful cat. Claws had been her closest friend until now. She did not make friends easily nor did she want any friends. The sudden attachment she had developed for Jusef was totally out of character for her. She was more aloof, independent and unattached, preferring the unemotional character of her cat. Better not to worry about the persons of interest she spied on for Agent Huber. Why was he so interested in Jusef?

A voice came through the door again, "Tatiana, I know you're in there!"

She huddled in the corner with her knees under her chin caressing her cat, thinking, if I can't see him, maybe he'll go away. They warned Tatiana from the time she was recruited: *There will be hard times; you must be strong and committed. You must keep your promise to us so we can trust you. You are our eyes and ears; without you, our mission becomes more difficult. When approached, react in the following manner. Deny any accusations made against you. Resist the offer to cooperate. Appear frightened, and then agree to spy for the FBI and become their informant. Develop a bond of trust with them. Interpret anything they assign to you. Be truthful in the beginning, and cultivate a relationship with your handler in order to obtain as much information as possible.*

Lazar reminded her, *"All Westerners are corrupt and believe anyone will do anything for money or to save himself according to this belief in all dealings. Did they not have a traitor named Hammond in their own organization? He was not tried for treason because the FBI would look bad. Where is the concern for National Security when one of their own is involved? The Bureau never found any traitors in the ranks, but somehow the CIA found Hammond within months. Hammond was even allowed to keep his pension."*

Tatiana wondered if Bob bugged her apartment. Did he have hidden cameras installed? She never considered him a threat, this straight-laced, academic-looking government official. Those are the ones to watch. Tatiana told Lazar she never imagined secret police in America could be so starched and ironed as this guy. Reluctantly, she opened the door.

"Bob," she greeted, "I didn't mean to delay, I was just getting dressed for work—I'm running late because I had too much to drink last night."

Her handler displayed his displeasure with angry eyes, red face and a vein protruding alongside his forehead. Seeing the irate agent framed in the doorway, she instantly broke into laughter, which caused another vein to pop out from his neck. He peered past her into the room, checking out her story.

"And how is FBI Special Agent Bob this morning?" she coyly asked.

"Why the hell didn't you open the door? Is there someone in here with you?"

Defiantly, she came back, "You should know. You've probably got my whole place bugged."

Pushing past her into the room, he continued searching and interrogating, "Have you had any contact with your new friend?"

"Umm, I don't know where he is; I was kind of hoping he would call me," she replied, "but I haven't heard anything as yet!"

"I know. We haven't been able to locate him either," he officially proclaimed. "Get ready. I'll take you to work."

"If *we* need to find him, shouldn't you check that neighborhood where we dropped him off?" she sarcastically suggested.

Ignoring the smart ass, Bob pulled off his glasses and went on, "I'm serious, Ms. T. I can tell you that getting him to talk to us could be financially advantageous to you!"

She turned her head and rolled her eyes. Bob went by the book when the formula came to getting more information from people. Tatiana knew how to convince him she would act as bait and capture the prize.

His training manual called for a planned meeting in a secluded place where he could pick her brain. Offer a $10,000 bribe for a successful mission, a textbook case. The agent desperately needed Tatiana to uncover this person of interest for his report. She would surely come through. Her information had been reliable up to now.

Since providing Tatiana as a sacrificial lamb to the FBI, Lazar was free to concentrate on planning and logistics. Unaware of all Lazar's activities, Bob was busy tracking down the new informant's steady supply of misinformation. The suspected terrorists' unexpected appearance and abrupt disappearance turned Bob's entire attention to pursuing Jusef.

"Tatiana, I really need your help to find him," he insisted.

Lately, Bob had failed to provide his superiors with credible information, making him anxious. Months passed since Washington had received anything of value. His superiors grew impatient to the point of instructing him to start producing substantive 302 reports or face being transferred. Last week, noting no sign of improvement in the quality of his work, Cleveland's Special Agent in Charge called Bob in to his office. The supervisor warned this was his last chance.

His informer came in from the bedroom dressed in a short black skirt with matching leather boots and a tight red sweater that clung to her ample breasts. Compelled to comment on her attire, he quizzed, "Are you going to work or out on a date?"

"I am going man hunting. How do you like the bait?" she said, spinning in front of him to display her charms.

"He doesn't have a chance. I'm glad you are on our side."

From his blue Ford pick up truck across the street, Bugs monitored Tatiana and Bob approach. One of several concealed lenses recorded their activity on his equipment in the van. Bugs smiled at the moving picture that projected the image of a prostitute and her john, thinking what the agency would not do to make a case—*better Huber than me*. She adjusted the fluffy collar on her three-quarter-length fur coat to protect her face from the blustery snow. Pulling leather gloves over her slender fingers, she climbed up into the truck.

On their way to the bookstore, he watched the made up little snitch from the corner of his eye. Bob was having doubts about her loyalty, evident from her cold demeanor, unusual quiet and casual attitude about locating Jusef. Her skirt had ridden up past mid thigh when she entered the truck. Tugging at the hem and pulling her skirt lower to the knee line turned him on.

The inclement weather and descending darkness brought an abnormal quiet for a Friday to this part of town. The approaching winter storm added to the uneasiness. A silent twenty-minute ride included a drive by search of the area where Jusef was last sighted. He could not put his finger on it, but something was wrong. Her silence aroused more suspicion than reassurance as he left her off at the store.

At the sight of her outfit, fellow employees greeted her with a stare. As she rushed from the truck into the store, the ring tone *Masquerade* played on her phone. She quickly ducked into the back room, anxious at the possibility Jusef was calling.

"Yes?" she asked.

"Mr. Lazar needs to see you," a serious voice said.

As if someone might be listening, she shoved the phone in her pocket and opened the door a crack to peek out into the store, half expecting someone had been sent to spy on her. Sighing, the coast was clear. She walked to the front window and looked up and down the street—not a living soul in either direction, most especially Bob.

She retrieved the phone from her coat pocket, "Just a minute, I'm at work. Our federal friend dropped me off. I suspect that he is watching me right now. Can I get a number to call you back?"

The voice instructed her, "This time, order a pepperoni pizza with goat cheese from the Middle Eastern Pizza Shop."

The November Storm picked up intensity as winds hurled large wet snowflakes against the protective front windows. The frozen crystals melted on the glass turning into liquid drops running down the warm surface in rivulets. She hoped Jusef was safe from the storm and Huber.

Finally free for the moment, Tatiana heard the store phone ring. She was surprised to hear Bob's voice. Silently, she fretted— *now what?*

"Have you heard from our friend?" the annoying voice inquired.

Attempting to mask her irritation, she nonchalantly replied, "Not a word; but when I do you'll be the first to know. Have you checked for him at the hospitals or places like that?"

His demanding tone projected disgust, "Just call me if you find out anything, I'll be waiting and watching!"

"I know. You've got the whole place bugged."

"No. But, I worry about you."

"Thanks. I'll call you as soon as I hear anything. Good bye."

Bob started thinking about the pole camera. Could they have recorded any worthwhile? He immediately dialed his technician back at the surveillance van.

Bugs reported, "Nothing new—according to the log, the last entry had the girl and the subject in the apartment for five hours the night before they left with you. Both appeared intoxicated when they entered. She never left after you took her home. No other unusual activity was visible until she left today with you."

Bob's brow furrowed on cue, an outward sign of his anxiety. The fish and the snitch participated in a Halloween party, left under the influence of alcohol and stayed together 5 hours in Tatiana's apartment. He doesn't fit the profile.

16 | PIZZA GUY

JUSEF'S CHARACTER HAS CERTAINLY CHANGED. I CANNOT GET OVER how quickly he snapped. He acted completely insane when he attacked our family like a madman and ran off with Ali. He may have been brainwashed. Nonetheless, I still want to help Jusef. I am afraid he has turned his back on the family. The time for finding him without consequence is over. I informed my nephew Gabriel of our encounter with the terrorist, "Tonight, Lt. Popovich killed an arsonist possibly linked to our search."

"A shooting; I could have been there," an energized Gabriel shouted over the phone.

"Calm down. This is not a computer game; someone is dead." I continued, "We have been checking on a few people, along with some storefronts, vehicles and transit stops. You should start back for the train platform, soon. We will meet you there. Be careful. Do not do anything on your own."

"I will look for him at some of the other stations on the way; the train is here now. I will meet you at East 105," he said, breaking into a run.

"See you later."

I returned my attention to my colleagues. The newly formed three-man international anti-terrorist team set out to locate the two suspects. The mounting evidence began to point toward an imminent attack. Our mission is to stop the assault and Jusef before he ends up dead. My colleagues provided invaluable assistance with their contacts in my quest. They have covered their tracks, but not vanished. We can be certain no one swallowed them up; both are probably hiding in plain view with new identities. Who are they now?

After a fruitless search, I suggested, "The weather is becoming worse by the minute."

"The fish are not biting," Jay mused.

"We must pick up Gabriel. He claims to have seen four of the terrorists on campus," I informed my colleagues.

"This may be the break in our case. Let's go. We can check for Jusef on the way."

"They may have discovered we are on to them," I concluded.

Five minutes later, Tatiana phoned her request in to the Pizza Man.

He said, "Wait ten minutes, then walk out back. Come alone!"

She watched the second hand sweep away ten minutes, and slipped out the back door.

The back alley is dark, where is he? Tatiana pondered. A battered van with lights out crept into sight and came toward her. The black van with a pizza decal on its side stopped three feet from her as the side door silently slid open.

A stern voice reassured and then commanded, "Don't be afraid. Get in."

She ducked in out of the weather. The aroma of Pepperoni pizza overwhelmed her senses. As the truck lurched forward, Tatiana braced herself against an inside panel. The lights remained off until the driver felt safe. No surveillance vehicles in sight. Brushing the snow from her sleeves, she anxiously surveyed the interior with the hope of finding Jusef. Turning and squinting, her eyes adjusted to the darkness, focusing on two males in front and a third seated in a chair in back. A dim light from a five-inch portable TV flooded the compartment. Pizza boxes and empty plastic milk crates surrounded her. She sat on of the crates, face to face with a man in an overstuffed green leather recliner.

She asked where they were going, as the driver maneuvered the van over snow-covered streets. Street lighting slightly improved the interior visibility, revealing her furrowed eyebrows in a glint of fear. She recognized the man in the improvised CEO chair.

She spoke up again, "Mr. Lazar, where are we going?"

Leaning forward, he silently glared.

Angrily, she demanded, "What did you do with him?"

"To whom are you referring?" he responded in Arabic.

"Jusef—he has done nothing wrong," she implored.

"—Jusef who? I know many with the name Jusef," he answered.

"You know who I mean." She continued, "Please listen to me. I'm in trouble with the FBI. I trusted you. Why do you now play games with me?"

"We have been doing this a long time. You are still learning. This is no time to deviate from our plan. We must stay the course. Patience is our ally. Bin Laden has shown us the U.S. Government is corrupt and self-destructive. Let me remind you, the Americans' secret police are more worried about their reputation than the security of their country!"

He continued, "How do I know you have not been compromised? Where do your loyalties lay, with your new love or with us? Who can trust a young woman involved with a man that she knows nothing about? I only requested that you test his loyalty. You have put us all at risk!"

"What have you done with him?" she repeated.

"How do you know this Jusef is not working for the FBI?"

"My handler and the agency consider him a *person of interest*. FBI agents are looking for him and have offered me a ten thousand dollar reward."

"Individuals are not important. There are rules that must be followed closely to survive in this game. The wrong move will end your life. Is this understood?" Lazar's voice sounded threatening.

"Yes, I understand. I swear to you he is a good soldier, and one of your most loyal."

Ignoring her, Lazar ordered, "From now on, all communications will be through our contact at the Zanzibar. Now go. Remember, your FBI friend is monitoring your actions. For the moment, you have slipped from his grasp, but must remain on guard. Is this clear?"

"Yes."

"Yes, what?"

"Yes, all is clear. If I discover Jusef cannot be trusted, you will be the first to know."

The pizza van climbed the hill on Mayfield Road past the quarry-stone wall behind Lakeview Cemetery. Yassar cautioned her to keep out of sight. He turned onto a side street and stopped to let Tatiana out.

On the way to Coventry, Tatiana's pace slowed through the wet snow as worry overtook her. She formed a plan to evade Bob and prevent discovery by mingling with the evening crowd. She looked back over her shoulder to observe the taillights had disappeared. *How could I not have seen the signs? Was it when my parents converted to Islam? Was it Lazar springing me from the first trap?* She wavered between expressing gratitude and skepticism for this cunning manipulator. *What was I thinking? How did I become involved with all these persons of interest? Khalid, the Saudi Engineering student at Case University, who claimed he was falling in love, had introduced me to the Lizard's phony charities. Was Khalid truthful or only acting to gain my trust as part of Lazar's master plan? Then, my dear friend Special Agent Huber, with his false promises of immunity, quickly threatens me with imprisonment if I did not perform as directed. Was there no way out?*

Following her parents conversion to Islam, they left Cleveland, preferring the Muslim community in Detroit. Ostracized for remaining loyal to her Christian upbringing, she was cut off from the tuition and allowance. Her father threatened never to speak to her again except to deliver his parting words: *If you desire to be a liberated woman, you would surely want to pay your own way.*

In the beginning, Khalid cheered her up. The class comedian intentionally mispronounced words in French class, amusing her and other students. His antics made her troubles vanish. The new relationship flourished until the young suitor attempted to persuade her to date him exclusively. When he suggested she quit her job and promised to take care of her, she was enraged. From the beginning, her financial plight stood in the way of their relationship. She repeatedly refused his offers of assistance with an iron resolve. *I slept with Khalid because of my feelings for him, not his money.* Her repeated refusals frustrated Khalid, providing a constant source of arguments. Determined to help his lover, he introduced her to wealthy friend Tarik Lazar.

Was I that naïve or did I blindly trust Khalid and his friend? Mr. Lazar and his associates donated heavily to Islamic charities. *At the time, I had no reason to doubt Lazar's story.* Many generous persons donate anonymously to charities. He told me about their acts of mercy to widows and orphans. His generous offer seemed a godsend at the time, considering my lack of options. *I reluctantly agreed to deliver money to a post office box in New York City for the extra income.*

I should have been suspicious on the first trip when Khalid picked me up in the rental car, and drove to the bus terminal in Erie, Pennsylvania. He explained that travel in New York City would be easier by bus because traffic and parking were terrible. When we arrived at the post office, he led me to an area with hundreds of post office boxes. Khalid quickly unlocked one of the doors and stashed the duffel. Obviously, this was not his first trip. On the ride home, Khalid handed me an envelope, "for services rendered, next time you will be alone." *I felt like a drug courier.*

The uneventful trips that followed involved a different vehicle and a new PO Box number. The routine bored me after traveling so many times on the same route and destination. At first, she missed Khalid and his companionship, but he had soon disappeared after their first excursion. *I wonder, was he really from a wealthy family, did he truly care for me or was I his replacement? Occasionally my conscience troubled me about where these donations came from.* Most importantly, where were the bags of money going, to whom and for what purpose? Once, she actually protested to Mr. Lazar and attempted to put an end to the monthly journeys, dumbfounded when he casually threatened to have her put in prison for her illegal activities. Shortly after that conversation, a monster of a man with deformed hands approached in front of her apartment and advised that continuing the deliveries and doing whatever told was in her best interest.

My quiet routine ended the day three black sport utility vehicles came out of nowhere and boxed me in as I drove into the Erie Bus Terminal parking lot. A black clad gang of armed ninjas appeared from every direction. The agents pointed guns at me through the windows of my Ford Taurus.

"FBI, don't move, keep your hands where we can see them!" they growled.

One ninja yanked her from behind the wheel and slammed her against the car while another searched and handcuffed.

"You are under arrest," he said, as the ratchets in the cuffs clicked closed.

"I got the money," shouted another, holding up the bag.

Rushing me to one of their vehicles and driving to an undisclosed location, I was sandwiched between two of the men in black. As the black truck entered a garage connected to several offices, they discussed bringing me in for questioning. This was my first encounter with Special Agent Robert Huber.

"You are in serious trouble," he threatened, standing up from behind a desk. One of them removed a cuff from her left wrist and seated her in an office chair. The agent by the desk raised his hand, stopped the other, and asked if she was right or left-handed. She was right-handed. Huber signaled the interrogation would continue while the other agent cuffed her left hand to the chair, placed the backpack on a desk and left. A reality flashed in my mind—*I was alone with the bespeckled man.* He then pulled out the money and waved it in her face, issuing another threat, "Do you have any idea how much prison time you'll get for this? I am

Special Agent Robert Huber of the Federal Bureau of Investigation assigned to the Cleveland Office. Who were you transporting this money for?"

Tatiana did not answer. He again asked who gave her the cash and who was to meet her in New York. She mustered up the nerve to ask her interrogator, "Aren't you supposed to advise me of my rights and provide me a lawyer?"

"You watch too much television. Post nine-eleven, the rules were rewritten. Your ignorance is not my fault. The Patriot Act affords us new powers. We caught a runner funneling drug money. Right? That means about ten years, and life if the money can be traced to terrorists. Think hard about the consequences." He paused, allowing time for his words to sink in. Unaware of what was happening on the national stage, she found herself like most Americans, caught up in performing her daily duties. She failed to take interest in these erosions of individual liberty. As Huber put it, new laws targeted someone else, while she turned a blind eye. Now that those same laws applied to her, she wanted Constitutional Rights. "You are a very attractive young woman. Your life would be over by the time you get out of jail."

He spelled out her bleak situation: This was not a drama; his threats were real. She sat helplessly listening until the special agent slipped in the word *unless* to his conversation. The mere mention of the word kindled a spark of hope in her. With an uplifted spirit, she inquired, "Unless what?"

"Unless you cooperate."

"What do you want from me?"

"Information." The agent looked up, as if searching for his next words. "Think about this: Today, information is a commodity that we trade. If you cooperate in helping me collect information, I can help you. Are you interested?"

Agent Huber laid out what was expected of her. Tatiana was to report to him and provide names, details, contacts of targeted individuals that frequented the bookstore. If any others appeared on the agency's radar, report their actions, including Khalid and Lazar.

"What has Khalid done?"

"Nothing that we are aware of. At the moment, he is merely a person of interest."

"You think he's a terrorist?"

"I did not say that. Do you think he's a terrorist?" Tatiana did not respond. "You have to agree, he has interesting friends, and he has traveled extensively throughout the Middle East, Europe and Africa." Seeing a lag in her interest, he switched gears, "I am offering you a chance to help yourself. Are you willing to work for us?"

Tatiana stopped breathing. She had already decided to co-operate, but appearing too eager might not be in her best interest either. Was this her sole chance to escape serving a lengthy imprisonment? After re-establishing eye contact, she whispered, "Fine. I will do as you ask."

For over an hour, Huber tested her as his new informant by repeatedly asking questions about Khalid and Lazar. How did they meet, what were the names of all the players, how long was she delivering the money, were there any other drops, was cash the only commodity ever couriered, was anyone carrying weapons, were there any other locations drops… Over time, her FBI handler made things uncomfortable. He reiterated *discover the truth—it will set you free* (as long as you did what Huber wanted).

Tatiana opened up, "I only met Mr. Lazar on only two occasions. The first time was at Aladdin's restaurant, when Khalid introduced me and Tarik picked up the check. I agreed to deliver the money to his charities. The second time, several months later, I went to his store on the west side to ask not to deliver any more to his charities."

Huber sat back in his chair and stared with a question on his face.

She threw up her hands, "I know what you are thinking. He refused to let me quit. You were not there to see his black dagger eyes. He frightens me."

"How much are you paid for each delivery?"

"The first time Khalid handed me an envelope with a thousand dollars in twenty dollar bills."

"Do you know what they call twenty dollar bills?"

"I've heard the expression means *drug money*."

"How many other deliveries have you made?"

"This was the twelfth."

"How many times did Khalid accompany you?"

"Only on the first trip."

"Where is he now?"

"I don't know. Soon after, he disappeared, and I have no information as to his whereabouts."

Bob was developing his hostage into an informant. He sweetened their relationship, "There will be some perks for working with us."

"What kind of perks?" she asked.

He began to explain, "After awhile, if we see you are working out and provided your information is reliable, there will be some cash incentives, rewards and bonuses, or whatever you wish to call them. In most cases, you will not have to worry about the local police. I will be your contact to the agency in all matters. You are free to contact me at any time on my cell phone if anything important becomes known. By the way, there is some paperwork to fill out before you complete the delivery." He handed her the forms and a pen.

Handcuffed to the chair, she inquired, "You still want me to deliver the money?"

"Yes, the same as before—we don't want anyone to get suspicious of you. Actually, the entire routine is to be continued with one exception: that you inform me of everything you are asked to do, before you begin. Is that understood?"

"Yes."

"Are there any questions?"

"No."

The usual paperwork was completed as Tatiana signed her life away somewhere in Pennsylvania, or possibly Ohio—the state really didn't matter. The bureaucratic machine assigned a code name and number to her as she was logged into a computer like a piece of government property. Her brief thought of breaking free from the net vanished hours before the red tape was finished.

She never liked authoritarian figures. They reminded her too much of her father. On the other hand, Bob Huber was in a category all his own.

Bob reminded her of a World War II film Gestapo agent, depicting him as a heartless man without a conscience, protecting the state from all enemies. He was capable of anything. *Where do they find these people?* In the name of national security, the end always justifies the means, and more importantly, the state is protected. Secret agents all over the world fear the loss of government immunity and being held accountable for transgressions against people abroad and at home. The more time spent with her handler, the more she despised him. He responded by permitting her to address him as *Bob* if no one else was present. *How do I get untangled from this web?*

HANDLING THE HANDLER

A group of TV sets flashed the weather forecaster's warnings and storm updates across the screen as she passed a store window. *A trigger for some upcoming bad weather will come from an unusually severe southwestern front that will be here in a couple days…our normal Canadian low-pressure clippers from Alberta won't cause this weather event. This approaching storm may be the first big event this season. We'll keep you posted on its progress!*

An Acme Internet bulletin coincided with the TV weatherman's alert: *Storm Warning; severe weather front rapidly approaching; make necessary preparations; repeat, time for necessary preparations. All assigned personnel are to report to project worksites by 0100 hours. Preparations are to be completed by 0300 hours. No overtime will accrue.* The signal to strike had been sent.

The tune *Masquerade* drifted from Tatiana's purse for a second time. She checked the caller ID: Bob again. Ignoring his call, she placed the phone in her pocket, not wanting to be cut off from rapidly developing events.

Within five minutes, another call. She instantly looked at an unfamiliar number. She flipped open her phone, wondering who was calling.

"Hello? (Silence)—Hello is anyone there?"

"Hello. This is Jusef. I had to call. I have been thinking of you constantly. I must see you."

"I want to see you, too. I have been worried about you. I thought you lost my phone number—"

"I destroyed the note you gave me. Keeping the paper would not be wise, so I memorized the number. You could be in danger if this message was discovered."

"Are you in some kind of trouble?" she questioned.

"I cannot talk now. Can we meet someplace soon?"

"Say where."

"I am not familiar with this area. I do not know any safe locations."

"The train platform at 105 and Cedar has a coffee shop. I do not know how much time we can spend, but I want to see you. I am leaving now."

"So am I—"

Huber impatiently watched the front of the bookstore. Hours passed since Tatiana had entered. Why has she not contacted me? What was she up to? He made a call to pass the time.

Lazar's phone signaled a call. "Hello."

The excited Huber asked, "Tarik, I have not heard from you for weeks. What have you been up to?"

"I have been busy checking out information that may be of importance to you."

Disgusted, he threatened, "I should just arrest you for trafficking food stamps and money laundering. You haven't given me anything of importance for months."

"Are you familiar with the recent shopkeeper murders?"

"Yes? What about them?"

"All three may be connected—a professional hit ordered by people from Detroit."

"What does that have to do with the FBI?"

"Terrorists may be involved."

"Don't string me along. Do you have anything solid or not? Washington is beginning to doubt your importance to us based on the garbage you have given us lately. Your information is always old news or common knowledge; instead of local intelligence."

"Did I not give you the beautiful Tatiana gift wrapped?"

"You had better come up with something soon. Or else you will end up in a prison cell!"

"Yassar," Tarik called out to his driver, "I think Agent Huber hung up on me."

Both men laughed inside the van at Lizard's remark.

This is all a bunch of B.S., Bob thought as he charged into the bookstore. "Where is Tatiana?" he demanded. Bewildered, the elderly man behind the cash register looked up at him. Bob stopped himself before revealing his identity.

The salesman asked politely, "Who are you looking for?"

"Where is the girl with the long dark hair? She was supposed to locate a book for me."

"Maybe I can help you. Under what name was the book reserved?"

"I didn't leave a name. She was going to do a computer search and have the information when I returned. I did not place an order."

"She was here, but a relative took sick and she had to leave."

"That's alright. I'll check back next week. Oh, would you check and see if she left any messages?"

"No message, she received a phone call and asked to leave."

"How long ago was that?"

"Why do you ask?"

"I may have just missed her. Perhaps I can catch her."

"I doubt that. She left over an hour ago."

"Thanks," he remarked, stomping off toward the door.

"Have a nice evening, sir," the clerk called out as Bob stormed out.

Tatiana hurried from the bus and bounded the four concrete steps up to the platform walking directly into the coffee shop. Jusef shadowed her in from the waiting crowd. Inside, she took a seat at a small table by a fogged window. Startled by his sudden appearance, he sat across from her with a smile of satisfaction.

"I thought I would never see you again."

"I could not stay away. You sounded so desperate," she responded.

"I am. I do not know how to say this, but I will try. Do you mind if I continue in French?"

"Go on. I prefer French."

"To be honest with you, I am here to avenge the murders of my father and grandfather."

"Murdered by whom?"

"They were killed in wars. Grandfather was a policeman in Palestine killed during the early struggle in 1948. My father was a colonel in the Iraqi army killed by the Americans. I have come to claim justice for both of them."

"But how can you claim justice? What can you do?"

"I cannot say since that would only place you in danger. I care for you very much and was almost ready to abandon my mission for you. I am in love with you."

He continued speaking, until she reached across the table and silenced him with her fingers over his lips. He grasped her hand, "This sounds impossible. I know little of you, but my feelings run deeper than our lovemaking. They come from my heart—where you will always be no matter what happens tonight."

"What do you mean 'no matter what happens'?"

"I must finish what has been started. Many others are involved. I cannot let them down. What we are about to do is more than one act of revenge. We are going to strike a blow for all oppressed people and avenge our martyrs."

Calmly, she replied, "I know." Her two words stopped him cold as her hand reached across touching his, "I think I'm in love with you, too."

From across the table, their eyes embraced. He squeezed, then lifted her hands to his face and kissed the back of her right hand.

Puzzled he implored, "I do not understand."

"Let me say one word—Lizard."

As he released her hand at the mention of the name, his eyes bulged and his mouth popped open. "How is this?"

"I have known him and helped with certain matters for some time now."

"Why?"

"I told you my family came from Lebanon to escape the civil war in Beirut. My grandfather and his brothers fought the Turks, British and later the Israelis. My father grew up attending many funerals before coming to America. Father desired freedom and a new way of life in America. Several years ago, he began questioning the blind allegiance to Israel and abandoned his Christian faith to become Muslim. His radical friends at his mosque changed him. To please him, I signed on, to help people back home by delivering messages at the bookstore. Now I am an outcast from my own family and a double agent with no future and no way out. I also work for the FBI."

"That man, Bob—"

"He is my contact. He lets me get away with a lot. Actually, I think he likes me. I never planned to meet someone like you, so innocent and pure with a warrior's heart. I regret corrupting you the way I did."

"Not so—I was corrupted before I met you. I will finish my work and we will start a new life together in Switzerland."

Bob returned to his unmarked car from the bookstore and called Bugs. "She's fled the coop. Find her. I'll be using the black Monte Carlo." Bugs activated the locator on her phone. Within minutes, the computer had found her. The agent at tech control informed Bob that his subject was presently at East 105 and Cedar.

Even with the global positioning system dismantled, following Yassar's van from the bomb factory staging area left Ali terrified of being caught by the local police. Ali finally felt empowered, even if only in charge of an expensive piece of transportation. The smell of an unblemished Cadillac pleased his senses. He toyed with the power windows and radio scanning system, while exploring the endless gadgetry. Ali relied heavily upon Yassar's evasive driving patterns and knowledge of the city.

Struggling to keep his attention on operating the vehicle, he drove past a block of demolished houses. The sight caused a flashback to the devastating scene when he returned from school and found his Iraqi home bombed and discovered his parents had been killed along with the neighbors. His grip tightened around the steering wheel as feelings of revenge swelled up inside him. These flashbacks helped remind him why he was here. Once away from the devastated block, he regained his composure.

His thoughts returned to his new partner—Ahmed. He knew nothing of the stranger that would accompany him behind enemy lines. At least Ahmed spoke better English in case the enemy confronted them. From the beginning, Ali assumed that Jusef would be deployed along side him, but as a loyal soldier, he tacitly accepted the change in personnel.

The sparse traffic made the drive back to Lizard's Rock less than the odyssey he had conjured up. Following the van at the speed limit, along with the evasive route, helped restore his driving confidence. As Yassar parked behind the headquarters, he motioned for Ali to park around front.

Inside, he passed Lazar sending emails that Ali presumed were activating cells deployed in other locations throughout enemy territory. Arriving in the back room, he observed Yassar standing over a young man who knelt devoutly on a prayer rug. "This is Ahmed. He will assist with your assignment tonight." Without interruption, Ali joined his new comrade, offering praise to Allah. Both soldiers' pleaded in prayer for a successful mission.

17 | SIGHTSEERS

"Mikey?"

"McPherson here," the once proud Bridge Operator answered his phone.

"This is Sean Patrick from the Long Shoreman's Hall in Cleveland. They probably told you I'd be calling during night shift with a few questions. Do you have a minute?" he asked.

"Sure, I've got all night, except now we've got to 'jump' from bridge to bridge in our own vehicles. Isn't that a violation of our contract? We're down to three operators per shift, that's half of what we used to have. Someone's goin' to get killed out here one of these nights 'cause there's no one around to chase trespassers away."

"We'll get to all of that in about sixty seconds. I'm walking from my car now."

A tall slim 40-year-old man with red curly hair closed the door behind him in the 9 by 9 cubicle, pulling out his clipboard and pen to take notes from his interview.

"Doesn't the City of Cleveland have six manually operated bridges over the Cuyahoga River?" Mr. Patrick quizzed.

"That's right." Sean was trying to find out more about why the bridge operators were considered part of a special group among workers. "What are your biggest problems here on the river bridges?"

"Over the last several years, management has brought in a young four-eyed know-it-all field supervisor." McPherson explained how his nemesis was attacking the last of *the old crew*. "Thirty-two years ago, the City would never have dreamed of 'checking up' on us. Since they hired 'Mr. Know Nothing,' he's ordered us to remove any personal furniture and other property from our bridge offices. I've had to get rid of recliners, curtains, and televisions; you know, years ago, the City even helped us install antennas to improve our TV reception. This place is our *home away from home*; now he's even talking about making me lose weight and quit smoking—as if I'm offending somebody with my smoke. Who the hell's out here at night anyway?"

"Are you fit enough to do the work?" Sean asked.

"Hey, I can still climb up to the top of my bridge for inspections! He won't put me out to pasture like the rest of the old gang. They never replace any of the guys they force to retire."

"Mikey, co-workers say you are one of the most vigilant bridge operators, but your boss calls you a trouble-maker and a constant complainer."

"He doesn't even know our job!"

"What is your job?"

"We insure safe passage for river, land, and train traffic. We monitor all vehicle movement, assigning the appropriate right of way from our 'chicken coops.' These cable-operated bridges were developed to allow large ships in a narrow deep part of the Cuyahoga River to pass safely through a span of a mile or so up river to the Steel Mills. Take a look out there."

"I see from the lights," Sean said.

"These bridges by today's standards are obsolete but they still link East West crossings of the Cuyahoga River. During the busy boating season, lift and swing bridge operators make things easier for tall boats to get to Lake Erie and beyond from where they are docked along the river."

"Your boss says he's more worried about how your waistline is growing larger than your 32 years as a Bridge Operator. He even said that when you are bigger than the doorway to the bridge operator's office, he's firing you."

"If he thinks he can take on Michael McPherson, let him try!"

"He also said you are bigger than any two of the 24 Bridge Operators working for the Service Department."

"Yeah, maybe someone should tell him 'if it ain't broke, don't fix it.' We've worked for years guarding these 100-ton metal monsters. Our safety record speaks for itself."

"Well, I did make the man understand you have a superb record at avoiding crashes, caring and maintaining the structures, and moving traffic up river flawlessly. But maybe you made everything look too easy."

"They haven't come up with a technology that replaces human beings for this type of bridge work, not that they haven't tried. Over my career, the Bridge Operators Section has been cut to the bone while they double up our work at multiple bridges. Don't even mention that homeland security training crap we've been forced to attend since 9-1-1. One of these lonely nights, they'll be sorry."

"Well, let me get a chance to resolve some of this. The chief complaint, according to your boss was at times they can't reach you on your portable radio, so make sure you're always in communication."

"I know. I know. Listen, one of the last ships of the season is due tonight, so we'll have to talk later. Just ask them to give me back that easy chair. My old worn out chair was like a comfortable pair of shoes compared to the cold steel 'son-of-a-bitch' that they issued as a replacement."

"Stay warm."

"Later, man."

McPherson looked out into the night storm and listened to the cold air whistle through the old windows, naked from lack of curtains. The exposed shack left him vulnerable to the elements and visible to anyone who might be outside. Seeing his image reflected in the windowpane, he thought, I'm just a damned a sitting duck up here.

Storms usually did not affect bridge operation except for noise and visibility, which deteriorated by the minute. Most nights he could watch movies, news and read books on terrorism, constantly dreaming up how he would save the bridges from sabotage. At the risk of being fired, the hulking bridge operator came to work every day armed with a 25 caliber semi-automatic handgun concealed in his back pocket.

According to the movies, the conditions tonight seemed perfect for a bridge attack. His night vision binoculars felt useless with the sleet coming down. Even with the lights down and impaired visibility, the shadows grew more sinister outside the glass. Mikey focused on one of the cameras mounted above the window. He squinted to view an icy figure lurking around a bridge. Was the iceman real or just another shadow?

Ali parked their car under the shadow of the viaduct, peering at every opportunity for onlookers. A block away from the swing bridge, Ahmed went to the back and started unloading explosives from the trunk. Both men eagerly executed their rehearsed operations.

"Tonight, we are going to change the world forever and save civilization from the West's corrupt ways: narcotics, alcohol, and homosexuals," Ahmed remarked.

"Never mind changing the world; we must strike the eye of the beast and escape," Ali urged.

His comrade agreed, "We are fortunate to have been assigned to the Lizard's Brigade instead of a suicide unit. Now, we will be able to watch the fireworks and fight another day."

"Hurry, we need to blow these bridges and leave," Ali insisted.

His partner whispered, "Be quiet, someone is coming. No one is supposed to be here but us." Ahmed withdrew a 9mm from his coat pocket.

Ali placed his hand on Ahmed's forearm, cautioning, "Make sure he is not one of our people."

That's that—I'm going to check this out. There should be no traffic, radio or other activity tonight except for our late ship. McPherson was cautious, knowing how dangerous the flats were at night, especially the deserted areas along the east and west banks. He chambered a round in his gun, slowly climbed out of his nest, slid behind the wheel of his truck and sped down Old River Road toward the lake as freezing rain pounded his windshield.

"We've got some sightseers under the bridge," he called out on the radio.

"Which one," another operator requested?

"I'm leaving my coop and heading for the Center Street Bridge," he responded as he prowled the deserted street scanning for any suspicious movements or vehicles.

"How can you see anything?" the other operator chimed in.

McPherson responded, "Actually, the only movements I see on the monitor are shadows. That's why I'm going."

"Okay, keep me posted."

Approaching the swing bridge, he turned off his lights and pulled his truck off to the side near where he saw the iceman. Cautiously exiting the vehicle, he approached the unattended red swing bridge on foot, pistol at ready. "I'm here for you now, baby," he said to his beloved bridge, never considering the awaiting danger.

Sleet was plastering a slick coating of ice on the sidewalks and surfaces of vehicles. An unfamiliar Cadillac was parked nearby with footprints leading to the bridge. Following the footprints down the slippery bank under the bridge, he gave his last radio message, whispering, "I'm at the bridge. Somebody's down there." Nervously re-cocking his pistol, ejecting a live round, he shut off his radio to avoid giving away his position.

"What did you say?" the other operator asked.

No one answered.

The iceman was real, crouched behind the bridge support, watching the approaching figure. What appeared was a rotund man, moving toward the side of the bridge for cover, when his right leg slipped on the icy bank, throwing him onto his back. The gun discharged and flew out of his hand with a loud echo, rolling across the ice and over the edge.

"Oh, shit!" Mikey muttered, sliding down the bank. Frantically, he kicked and clawed at the earth in an attempt to stop backsliding into the river. Halfway down the slick incline, he was able to gain enough traction to stop. Slowly rolling over, he began to climb up the embankment on all fours with utmost care. One wrong move and he would be swimming with the fishes. As the struggling figure neared safety at the top, someone jumped him from behind and held his face to the ground. He felt an object pressed to the back of his head.

Whack! A stern blow to the bridge operator's head brought stars to his eyes. Remembering nothing until consciousness returned, he rolled around with the sensation of being an oversized load in a wash machine. He awoke bound in a cramped, dark space.

"Holy crap, I'm tied up in a car trunk! Good thing I let the crew know where I went," he mumbled through duct-taped lips as if the crew could hear him.

"Mikey? McPherson? Where are you?" the Carter Road Bridge Operator called out over the radio. *No reply on his cell phone, either. I hope that asshole didn't fall asleep in his truck again. I remember him saying how much more comfortable his truck was than that damned City-Issued Chair.*

"Third street operator here," the tender answered.

McPherson didn't answer his radio or cell phone for over twenty minutes. *I should report this to Four-Eyes if he doesn't answer. I'm not getting suspended for leaving my bridges to look for him. Something's wrong. He should have answered by now. He always answers— eventually.*

"Look. Allah has sent us a gift. We have their communications," Ali said, handing over their prisoner's portable radio and cell phone to his partner.

Again the voice came over the radio, "Mikey, where are you?"

As Ahmed held out his hands to accept the equipment, the captive's cell phone rang, startling the abductors. "Do not answer that," Ali snapped at Ahmed.

Simultaneously, the radio blared, "Mikey, are you alright? If you can't talk, just key the radio."

Ali looked at Ahmed, "Do you understand? I do not speak English so well."

Ahmed shrugged in the negative.

"Find out from the fat one how radio operates." Both kidnappers donned their ski masks before opening the trunk. Mikey McPherson started kicking at them immediately when the hatch opened, but surrendered the instant a black-gloved hand pointed a 9mm in his face.

"Your resistance is useless," Ahmed said.

The captive quit struggling against the duct tape on his wrists. He frantically looked around, searching for an opportunity to escape. Ali pulled the tape from McPherson's mouth.

"Find out what he was doing here," Ali requested of Ahmed in Arabic.

"You damn Arab terrorists. You won't get away with this!"

Ahmed asked in proper English, "Who are you? What are doing here?"

"I'm Michael McPherson, Cleveland Bridge Operator; who are *you* and what are *you* doing under *my* bridge?"

His captors laughed.

"You wouldn't laugh if my arms weren't taped up. There's a ship coming up the river in a few minutes and when I don't give the signal to open the bridge, you'll be caught."

"Show us the bridge, fatso," Ahmed commanded.

"I ain't telling you nuthin'."

"You already told us what we need to know," Ahmed mocked as he slammed the trunk lid shut and drove off, retracing the tire tracks in the snow.

The trail led them to the Columbus Road Bridge, where the kidnappers pulled the big man out of the trunk. Faces still covered, they marched him toward the bridge. At the same time, both scanned the area. No one appeared to be in sight.

The defiant prisoner boasted, "You'd better hurry up. The 'Master of the Lakes' is due any minute and the Captain will be calling with a request to lift the bridge." His captors forced him to climb back up into his control station without the use of his hands, a task for which they hadn't planned. Their efforts were like pushing an elephant up a ladder.

Panting and puffing up the slippery steps, he kept hoping for a chance to push these guys into the river. They secured their prisoner to a metal chair with duct tape once inside the bridge office. A long blast from the ship's foghorn cut through the sleet.

Mikey gloated, "The ship is requesting clearance to pass under the bridge. If I don't return his signal and raise the bridge, he'll call the port authority."

Ali picked up his pistol and raised the gun to the bound man's head, "No mistakes! Tell ship all is okay; show me controls! No mistakes!" Ali pressed the barrel to his prisoner's temple.

The reluctant hero identified which button to push. Ali gave two short blasts and the bridge started up. The ship responded with another long blast, a signal that meant everything was okay.

"Say what is usual!" Ali commanded, holding the radio to the bound man.

The bridge radioed the ship's wheelhouse, "You're late!"

A voice responded, "Really bad out on the Lake, glad we're on the river." As the ship began passing under the bridge, Ali grabbed the other lever and pulled back. The bridge started to descend.

"Hey, what are you doing...stop the bridge you crazy bastards, we'll all be killed!" Mikey yelled as he desperately tried to free himself from the chair. His captors bailed out of the office, down the bridge stairway, running along a catwalk between the metal pillars to a maintenance ladder where they made their escape.

A horrified voice from the ship's radio cried out, "—Bridge! Stop the bridge! Somebody stop the bridge!"

18 | EMERGENCY

Sounds of tearing metal screamed through the valley as the two monsters collided. While the ship's powerful engines continued to churn up the black river water, forcing the wheelhouse into the ship's bridge, Mikey's beloved bridge had been turned into a terrorist weapon. Each operator thought of a distress signal to call out but now was too late. This was a horrible way to see his bridges destroyed. Her death rattle shrieked over the November winds. Both steel giants were ripping each other apart; beam-by-beam and bolt-by-bolt. Tattered green pieces of steel from the bridge were spilling onto the ore boat and into the river. The lift bridge bent, buckled, and broke off, crashing into the deck and the frigid waters below. Ramming into the bridge, the impact sheared and plunged the ship's wheelhouse from the rusty deck. Confused sailors heard an unfamiliar splash as the ship bridge plunged overboard into the cold black water, with the men trapped inside. Only the bottom compartments and the engine were spared. Crewmembers, jolted from their quarters, rushed to the deck, bewildered and scrambling around in circles. They were struck with disbelief, not knowing what to do. The entire top section of the ship was gone: bridge, wheelhouse, communications and the officers were missing. The remaining crew was emotionally frozen unable to react.

One crew member ran back and forth on the deck with a spotlight as he searched the river for his shipmates. The solitary finger of light pierced through the black night only to discover twisted sections of the Lift Bridge scattered along the deck and shore. There were no visible signs of any survivors, not even a trace of the wheelhouse. The icy Cuyahoga had swallowed them. No training could have prepared the crewmen or operators for this.

Someone screamed, "Stop the ship!"

"How? The wheelhouse is gone," another voice shouted from the darkness.

"Go to the engine room and tell them to stop the engines, quick!" One of the men ran to the ladder way. The crew began to respond. The only ones hearing the deafening sounds of the collision were the terrorists, their victims and a second Bridge Operator named John. What was left of the dying bridge continued to moan and groan at its rusty joints. Brittle metal bent and cracked as each section broke free. The mighty steel cables made a pinging noise of a musical instrument that snapped a string. The mangled bridge columns that remained standing resembled large stalks of celery with their ends chewed off, the only remaining evidence that there ever was a bridge. The colossal noise startled John the operator in his coop.

What the hell was that; an explosion, a train wreck, or a bridge collapse? I'd better check on fat boy, I haven't heard from him for a while. John called out on the radio, "Mikey, where are you? Mikey; come in Mikey!" Dead silence. John tried his cell phone again. No answer. "I'm calling the police!"

As arctic winds began changing the sleet into snowflakes, the Police Radio announced: "Any car in the vicinity of the Eagle Road Bridge, check on a report of an explosion or large crash."

"Car three-one-one responding."

"Car three-one-three will start up that way." A few minutes passed before radio was advised of the situation by the first car to arrive on the scene.

"Car three-one-one on scene. Looks like the ship hit the bridge, which landed on the deck. Send us a boat and a helicopter; we need to get onto the ship to see what happened. Start a supervisor and get us the Fire Department and medical assistance!"

Dispatch responded, "Supervisor, Fire and EMS are responding; CPD Boats and Helicopters are not available; I made contact with the Coast Guard and they're notifying Detroit. This will take a while."

The ship's crew implemented damage control procedures and continued their search for survivors. They checked for further damage to prevent the ship from sinking. Meanwhile, teams of rescuers searched the deck for casualties in the midst of the destruction. One heard a desperate voice cry out, "Help, get me out of here, get me out of this damned chair!"

The sailor responded, "I can't see you, where are you?"

"Over here, over here, help; get me out of here." The beam from the flashlight located the frantic voice coming from a rectangular steel box, resting on its side. He peered in with a flashlight through one of the broken windows to find an overweight man taped to a chair on its back attempting to wiggle his way out. Under any other circumstances a fat man stuck in a chair would be comical. The rescuer weaved his way through the tangled wreckage to the far side of the green metal cage. He found the steel door had sprung open on impact.

Another crewman quickly came to assist, as Mikey repeated, "Get me the hell out of here." The first of several rescue vehicles began arriving on the scene while distant sirens wailed their approach.

One of the crewmen cut the big man free, the other commenting, "Good thing they taped you to such a sturdy chair—this probably saved your life!"

Helping him to his feet, Mikey facetiously affirmed, "Yeah, sure!" As he raised his voice, he sounded the alarm, "The terrorists are here—they murdered my bridge."

As his rescuers led him through the debris to the starboard side, he observed the devastation, and remarked, "Thank God, I'm alive!" He called out to the rescuers on the shore, "We've been attacked by terrorists; we need CPD!"

One of the obscured figures on the shore yelled back, "Cleveland Police; we're here; what happened?"

"Terrorists, I know there are at least two of them, maybe more. They put something under the swing bridge and jumped me. I think they're gonna blow the bridges up!"

"—With bombs?"

"Yeah, I'm telling you, I saw two guys putting charges under the bridges!"

"Are you sure?" the officer asked with skepticism.

"Only a bomb can do what the hell they did here! They stole my radio and cell phone!"

The Lieutenant jumped back into his car, "Radio, I'm going to channel seven."

Dispatch replied on channel seven, "Go ahead with your traffic."

"We have a witness who states the bridge and ship collision was done intentionally. Terrorists may have planted a bomb under another bridge. Notify the bomb squad and get a detective team over here on the double. Advise all cars their radios may detonate the bombs."

Radio acknowledged, "We're going to all channels to locate the units you request."

The dispatcher put out a citywide broadcast several times, but none of the special units responded. She gave the bad news to the Lieutenant on scene.

"That is negative on the bomb squad, sir!"

The Lieutenant quickly responded, "Contact the SIU Superintendent; have him bring a bomb crew in and advise them to report to me!"

Mikey observed that the top of ore boat had been sheared off and the remaining hull had ground to a halt, smashed and disabled. He looked for a way to get back on shore. A light from an approaching boat made its way around Collision Bend. He did a double take. Mikey thought, *how about that, they pressed the Fire*

Boat Anthony J. Celebreeze into service: They'll get me to shore. I can tell them what's going on. He borrowed a phone from the crew to call John. "Hey, John is that you?"

"Of, course you idiot! What the hell did you do, McPherson, wreck the bridge?" his counterpart called out.

"Keep your head down, terrorists took over my bridge; Two hooded masked men jumped me. They're armed and planting bombs under our bridges," Mikey warned.

John started out, "Come on man, don't—"

Mikey cut him off, "Listen man! I'm serious! We're under attack. They're after our bridges!" His fellow bridge operator didn't know what to make of this, but went along with him since he sounded so shook up. "We called 9-1-1 when I escaped from two guys who took over our bridge. They crashed the ship after they tied me to that fucked up chair. The cops are here, but we've got a lot of injured and missing crew in the river; including the Captain!"

John asked, "You okay?"

"I'll be fine, but be careful they're terrorists and they've got bombs and they're going to blow our bridges."

The Lieutenant waited on shore as the firemen commenced their rescue. They took the would-be hero and some of the injured crew to waiting paramedics on shore. Lieutenant Kilbane rushed over to the survivors coming off the fireboat, "Are you the bridge operator?"

"Yeah, I saw everything. I'm the one they jumped! They put something under the swing bridge," Mikey exclaimed.

"Settle down, tell me what happened first," Kilbane requested.

"I'm telling you, Lieutenant; you need to get down there. Terrorists are going to blow the bridges up!"

As soon as the officers assigned to Car 313 overheard the word 'terrorists', they jumped into action and sped to Old River Road to capture the saboteurs and save the bridge. Upon arriving, the officers observed a hooded figure walking under the swing bridge, footprints leading from a parked car.

The officer behind the wheel of Car 313 said, "We'd better get back-up!" His partner keyed the microphone. As he transmitted, several loud explosions popped their ears.

The driver yelled, "What the hell???"

The officer with microphone still in hand explained, "This is three-one-three! Some guy at the swing bridge just blew himself up! Another suspect fled, we'll be in foot pursuit. Get us some help!"

Another explosion echoed down river.

The rookie screamed into the microphone, "Three thirteen, the swing bridge just blew up." Huge pieces of metal and concrete were flying in every direction, crashing back to earth. The officers bailed out and ducked under their car to shield themselves from the aerial bombardment of debris. Reluctantly, they came out from under their black and white bunker, cautiously approaching the remains of the bridge, pistols at ready.

"Damn! What the hell is that?" one of officers asked. Their flashlights illuminated a body lying on the bank. They aimed at the lifeless figure as they continued their guarded approach. The second officer dropped back to cover the first.

"Holy shit; this guy is blown in half! Come look at this!"

The second officer questioned, "Where's his bottom half?"

"Jeez, he must have had a bomb strapped to him!"

His partner exclaimed, "I'll bet he's one of those suicide bombers!"

Another pair of eyes watched as two lovers kissed passionately on the train platform. Halogen beams illuminated the embracing couple, creating a theatrical atmosphere. They clutched each other, oblivious to the cold and falling snow. Looking on from the crowded bus stop, Agent Huber's hands trembled as his lower teeth bit his upper lip while observing the romantic scene across the street. Legs wobbling, he grabbed the handrail, and lowered himself onto the bench, his face flushed.

A short stout lady bundled in a red wool scarf and overcoat asked, "Hey mister, are you alright?"

"What's the matter with him?" a man next to her said.

Bob exhaled, "I'm fine. Today's been hectic. I just need to sit for a minute." He attempted to regain control of his emotions.

"This is about a woman, right?" the lady speculated.

Bob quickly glanced with a hard stare.

She continued to ask, "Is she that pretty girl across the street, kissing that man?"

"What makes you say that?"

"I'm sorry. This was none of my business."

"I should have known better. She made a fool of me after all the respect and freedom I allowed her," he thought.

She turned to the black man next to her. "These things always happen around Christmas. He should forget about her. He's a good-looking young man."

"Thank you," Bob responded.

As he stood up and watched the couple's pending departure, the strength came back to Bob's legs. The couple departed in separate directions. Jusef caressed Tatiana's face with his hand just before parting. Bob paused. Which one should I follow, he said to himself.

Unknowingly, Bob and Jusef simultaneously took one last look at Tatiana's long dark hair, sexy eyes and smile. Remembering her soft purring voice and girlish laugh, Bob calculated his next move.

On seeing Agent Huber start across East 105th Street, the stout lady called out to him, "Let her go." Bob ignored her suggestion and continued across the street.

Her faint 'be careful,' was drowned out in traffic.

Much as I want to go after her, I know Jusef is my target. She's still just another informant. I'll deal with her later, Bob mumbled to himself.

Tatiana took several steps before stopping to look back as Jusef faded from sight. She caught a glimpse of Bob and suspected he was following Jusef. She thought *that deceitful bastard is spying on me again! I thought I gave him the slip; I should have been more careful.* She fell in step twenty paces behind Jusef's pursuer. The cornflake-sized snow made both stalkers invisible to their prey.

Bob lost distance on Jusef and began following phantom footprints on the sidewalk. The gap between the footsteps was widening and the snow became more compacted into the pavement.

He's running! I can't let him get away. Fearing Jusef had evaded him; he too started running, when the suspect prints left the sidewalk into the park. At that moment, he decided to take him into custody.

He activated the voice command on his cell phone, yelling, "Get me some backup; I need help! I'm chasing two terrorists on—"

Bang!

Bob dropped his phone in the middle of his conversation. A sharp pain from one shot went through his right shoulder, knocking him to the ground.

Two loud blasts echoed! Immediately, a second and third bullet whistled above. He rolled several times across the ground and removed himself from the line of fire. Hours of survival training instinctively forced Bob to draw his weapon. Several more shots whizzed past.

He transferred the pistol to his good hand and immediately returned fire in bursts of two at the obscured silhouette. Following two or three loud cracks, a scream signaled at least one round hit the threatening shadow, knocking whoever fired to the ground. He sprang to his feet and cautiously approached the figure now laying face down and motionless in the snow. A large pool of dark red blood quickly formed along side the body, indicating the wounds may have been fatal. Automatically kicking the gun away from the suspect, he rolled his attacker over and looked into Tatiana's motionless eyes. He felt for her pulse and found no heartbeat. Desperately pushing his fingers more firmly against her neck, he checked again and again, nothing. A sudden wave of sadness overwhelmed him. Tears swelled as he stared at her face.

I wish that she had been a better shot. Bob grabbed his mobile, "Get me an ambulance!"

His back up requested, "Where are you? Our cameras can't see you through the snowfall—"

Bob cut off the other agent, "I'm in the woods, a thousand feet east of the train platform on East 105—"

Weapon still in hand, Bob fired at another ghostlike figure charging out of the snow.

Three cracking echoes! He fired until the phantom figure went down.

Bob shouted at his cell phone, "Get me some help; I just shot another one. He came out of nowhere."

A calming voice from the speeding undercover van responded, "Help is on the way."

Cautiously approaching, Bob yelled at the wounded suspect, "FBI, don't move!" The wounded subject was attempting to hobble away. Bob commanded, "I said freeze! FBI, if you move, I'll blow your head off!" The figure froze instantly, falling to his knees face down with arms outstretched on the sidewalk. Blood was oozing from the downed man's leg onto the snow. After cuffing the suspect, Bob checked for weapons and found none.

19 | UPDATES

Bɪʟʟ ᴅᴀsʜᴇᴅ ꜰʀᴏᴍ ᴀ ʀᴇᴅ ʙʀɪᴄᴋ ᴀᴘᴀʀᴛᴍᴇɴᴛ ʙᴜɪʟᴅɪɴɢ ᴀɴᴅ sʟɪᴅ into the rear seat of Jay's car. As we greeted, Jay questioned whether his partner was armed. Bill opened his jacket and informed us he was not packing. Officially, the case was off limits. On the other hand, a detective on administrative leave could still help a friend look for his *missing* nephew.

Jay reassured Bill, "Don't worry about Internal Affairs. I heard the case is going to be found justifiable. The ruling should come any day now, but that's off the record and you didn't hear this from me. Today, I also learned another dead body was discovered at the arson scene."

I pondered whether the fire was started to cover up another homicide. Was the homicide connected to our case or another random act of violence? Perhaps the video tapes were the arsonist's real target.

Bill interrupted my thoughts, "What do you think, Thomas?"

"I suspect the fire was set to destroy evidence." Both colleagues agreed with my deduction.

Jay updated his passengers, "In the event things heat up, there are two loaded shotguns in the trunk." He continued, "By the way, the dead guy's gun was taken in a Houston burglary."

Bill remarked, "That figures; they obtain a gun for one of their buddies in another city, and then an accomplice reports a theft so the terrorists get reimbursed by the insurance company."

"When was this weapon stolen?" I asked.

"Sometime last week," Jay reported.

"That weapon must have been fast-tracked," Bill exclaimed.

"We still have no positive identification on the dead suspect. However, while I was nosing around Homicide, they requested the body be re-fingerprinted at the morgue. Homicide is still trying to find out who the guy was: No identifying papers or marks, it's as if this guy fell out of nowhere," Jay revealed.

I inquired, "May we examine the body—we might discover something that was overlooked." Bill and Jay nodded their agreement to the idea, and within moments, we were driving east through gusts of blinding snow toward the county morgue.

In Cleveland, the striking contrast between neighborhoods brought to mind St. Pauli and the area around my apartment. Increased urban sprawl there coexists with stable neighborhood pockets despite ongoing changes. The St. Pauli I once knew is not the same. Then again, what is? Not all change is for the better. Sergeant Mayer had a solution: Consider moving. The advice was accepted in silence, knowing I couldn't relocate. I like the action and the people too much to move.

Bill mentioned, "We're coming up on University Circle, so keep an eye out for Gabriel. Besides, we may get lucky and spot Jusef."

"Jusef's probably shacked up, safe and warm," Jay noted. His thought seemed almost comical, owing to the severe weather conditions.

From what Gabriel tells me, there seems to be a lot of Middle Easterner foreign students in this part of town. As we strained our vision to search through a white haze for Jusef and the others, I concluded that Jay's hunch was a good one, but feared the companion was not necessarily female. The further east we drove, the fewer students appeared as snow piled heavier on the deserted campus.

We abandoned our impromptu search and turned onto a narrow driveway where floodlights illuminated a sign that read *Cuyahoga County Coroners Office*. The rear parking lot appeared empty save one other vehicle. Jay rang the bell at the back entrance to summon the night attendant. "Only a certain type of person can work here. What a creepy job." From the moment we entered, the indescribable scent of death permeated my senses, bringing to mind my own mortality. The attendant apparently recognized my colleagues, opened the door and silently motioned for us to follow toward the cooler compartments, where he slid the body out to examine.

Jay noted, "This cadaver was already posted and loosely sealed up."

The attendant picked at his half-eaten sandwich. Between bites, he inquired, "You want to view the other one from the store fire? He's badly burned, so we put him in the refrigerated room."

"Has the other body been posted?" Jay questioned.

"Not yet, but it looks like there's two bullet holes in him."

"We'll wait for the autopsy version."

I scrutinized the corpse of the arsonist who Bill shot and noted the lack of visible injury, considering the body had been hit with a car and then shot twice. The face was remarkably intact. From a vest pocket, I removed an envelope containing the seven photos along with my magnifying glass. Studying the face while comparing each photo, I turned and handed one of the photos to Jay, "This is him. Here is your gun courier." Bill and Jay studied the photograph and confirmed the match. "This man went from Hamburg to Cleveland, most likely through Houston, where he obtained the pistol."

"Just great! With all the other bullshit, we now have an active terrorist cell to deal with!" Bill lamented.

"To me, this looks as though you have more than one. Consider this: The organization stretches from Canada, to Mexico, to Germany, to Detroit, to Houston and to Cleveland, not to mention

Baghdad. Who knows where else? How many other cities and countries have active cells connected with this operation?"

"What the hell are they planning?" Jay reflected.

"Whatever it is, we don't have the resources to deal with this international threat. They could be planning to strike anywhere. Damn! We'll have to bring in the Feds," Bill conceded.

"Maybe now they will do something," I speculated. Now that I realized how the FBI tends to operate, my statement was merely a token gesture. Glancing toward Bill, I observed him rolling his eyes in disgust.

Jay punched in Huber's number on his phone and received a voice mail in reply. He left a message using a 9-1-1 to signal the terrorist threat and the need for an immediate response.

On our way toward the exit, I thanked the attendant. He came back with, "Do you guys want to see the stone that was in his pocket?"

Collectively, we stopped and turned around. In unrehearsed chorus we asked, "What stone?"

The attendant pulled out a cardboard box with the deceased's clothing and a brown envelope. While examining the clothing, I mentally noted that all garment labels or other identification had been removed. Bill opened the manila envelope, and turned it on edge, allowing a stone to roll out into his palm. I recognized the object for what it represented. "That is a Hajj stone."

"A what?" Bill asked, as he placed the object back in its property envelope.

As we returned to the vehicle, I shared a cultural lesson with my two friends. Based on first-hand experience acquired in the Middle East, I had become acquainted with Muslim customs, including the sacred pilgrimage to Mecca. On the last day of their journey, true believers throw their Hajj stones at the wall symbolizing Satan. Today, the United States is considered by many in the Middle East to be the Great Satan. Many Europeans believe the pentagon commenced a war based on lies, to spread their influence and corruption into the region. I stopped short of lecturing my colleagues on the subject.

When Jay's cell phone rang, Bill barked, "Now what—!"

"Sergeant Andrewski," Jay covered the phone's mouthpiece as he informed us one of his men was processing another homicide nearby. He took his hand away and continued to speak to the detective loud enough for us to overhear some of the pertinent details, "You say just past the 105 Train Platform there was an exchange of gunfire between an FBI Agent and two suspects; two Arab suspects? ... I see. The male is being treated along with the Agent at University Hospital. Has the dead body been moved? ... Okay, are the feds there yet?"

Hearing Jay say *Arab suspects* and *dead body*, I listened attentively to his every word, relieved to hear the most important question. My body tensed as I awaited the answer. Lord, please not my nephew.

"Do we have any additional info on the deceased?" Jay turned toward me with thumbs up, "Yes, the body is a female." Diverting his attention back on the caller, he explained that we would stop at the hospital before responding to the scene. Jay routinely placed his blue strobe light on the roof and we sped off.

In minutes, we arrived at U.H., a conglomeration of brick and concrete structures. On top of one of the taller buildings, a helicopter was landing on the roof. We passed under a glass enclosed pedestrian bridge that spanned Cornell St and turned onto the ramp leading to the ER. The hospital complex *city within a city* buzzed with activity.

Armed security approached our vehicle as Jay stopped his car next to two EMS units backed up to the Emergency Room doors. More than dozen marked and unmarked police units filled the parking area. The frustrated guard instructed us to park in the public lot. Jay backed up the ramp and left the car at the end of the driveway.

The distinct whirling sound of helicopter blades overhead caught all three of us instinctively looking skyward. Each carried personal thoughts about the circling chopper. Two minds returned briefly to Viet Nam, while the third conjured up memories from

Afghanistan. Jay reasoned that the noise was only a news chopper attempting a close up shot of the homicide scene, reminding himself this was not Nam.

Bill protested silently about his dislike of choppers, remembering being ferried into hot LZ's with his fellow marines. I reflected how NATO forces had depended on helicopters, especially around Kabul. Peering up toward the whirling bird from America's heartland, we stood in the midst of a war zone atmosphere.

I remarked to my comrades, "This one is very close."

"True, we are not far from the crime scene," Jay said.

Security challenged us at the door. We displayed our badges. They waved us through. Inside, the emergency room overflowed with chaos. Orderlies, nurses and an occasional doctor bumped into officers seeking information. Everyone acted as if he was running the show, but from all appearances, no one was in charge.

I stopped a nurse and inquired as to the gunshot victims' location. She eyed me suspiciously and did not answer my questions. After Jay flashed his badge, we learned that one victim, a young Arab, was in bed six while the wounded FBI agent was in bed five. Her quizzical gaze made me uncomfortable, but did not stop me from requesting permission to see the victim in number six.

"Are you his father?"

"No, but it is possible that we may be related," I responded.

"Not right now, this place is like a madhouse and another shooting victim is en route."

"Please, I have come a long way in search of my missing nephew—only a quick peek to see if it is my relative."

She turned and motioned us to follow down a crowded corridor, past the nurse's station to the triage area. Numbers above the stations identified the beds behind the cloth walls. She disappeared behind the curtain and we waited for her signal to enter. At last, we have found Jusef, I thought.

The nurse drew back the drape for us to enter. Seeing my nephew laying in the bed, I exclaimed, "Gabriel, what happened?"

"An FBI Agent shot me," he said excitedly in our native tongue.

Based on years of experience, I could tell the wound did not appear to be serious. A closer examination confirmed my first diagnosis: the bullet had gone through the leg without damaging any major artery and the doctors had stopped the bleeding. Bill and Jay too had expressed surprise to find Gabriel on the other side of the curtain.

As he looked over his propped leg, Gabriel explained that when his train departed the station at East 105, Jusef and a woman appeared on the platform. At that moment, he recognized his cousin. Unable to jump from the train, he rode to the next station and hopped onto a return train. In minutes, he sprinted from that train onto the deserted platform. Gabriel peered into the restaurant, then scanned the area to discover his only clue; a pair of fresh footprints in the snow. Instantly, he ran at full gallop, following the footprints until someone shot him without warning.

The doctor returned and reported the wound was through and through Gabriel's leg. The bullet had not broken any bones or arteries. He requested we leave to allow the staff to complete their work.

I squeezed my nephew's hand, to reassure him he need not worry. "One moment doctor," with all the excitement, I almost forgot—the photos. I presented them to Gabriel. Without hesitation, he positively identified four of the suspects as the males at the coffee shop. We embraced and I left.

I sat with Jay in a corner section of a waiting area away from the crowd. Bill took a coffee break in a vending machine area down the hall. An official noticed Jay and made his way to us.

"Chief, what's going on?" Jay asked.

Deputy Chief Gallagher updated Jay as I eavesdropped on their conversation. So far, the chief had learned the FBI was investigating a terrorist cell. One of their agents had been following two suspects, a male and female, for several days. Tonight, they met at an RTA Platform on East 105. The agent continued his surveillance on the male when the pair split up. Apparently, the suspect was on to the agent and began to run with the federal agent in pursuit, calling for backup. That was when the woman showed up and shot the agent in the back and he returned fire, killing her. The male came charging at the wounded agent, and he fired again, striking the suspect. That suspect is still alive and here at the hospital along with the wounded agent. "That's all we have so far."

"Chief, there's a lot more to this case than they're telling us," Jay said.

"There usually is when the *alphabet people* are involved," DC Gallagher retorted.

Jay informed the chief that we had proof that there is a major terrorist cell operating in Cleveland. Once he had the chief's attention, he introduced me and explained my involvement in the entire matter. The Deputy Chief and I shook hands as I spoke up, "With all due respect for the FBI, their agent mistakenly shot the wrong person." Now I had captured his undivided attention. I began to provide missing pieces to the puzzle the chief was attempting to piece together. Starting with the shooting of my nephew Gabriel, I handed the photo array to the Deputy Chief and updated him on how we had tracked the seven terrorists, including Jusef from Hamburg to Cleveland.

I expressed displeasure that Gabriel was shot while pursuing my other nephew. I pointed out Jusef's photo along with Ali's and added the fact they were in the US illegally. "Your two officers and I believe that all seven of these men are hiding in your city's Arab community." I again pointed to Jusef and Ali's photographs, "From when they entered the United States through Canada, and the others through Mexico, we traced all seven here. Gabriel positively identified four of these men after spotting them on campus. The fifth lies on a slab in the morgue, shot by Lieutenant Popovich. We also know that Jusef is here and are quite sure they are together. I believe they are ready to attack your country."

As he passed the photos to Jay, Gallagher asked, "Who else knows about this?"

Jay answered, "Right now, nobody but us and now you—we only identified him at the morgue a half hour ago from Thomas' photos."

"They never informed CPD of any ongoing investigation with this cell. We've got to let the Chief know what's going on," the DC said.

"Are the federal agents aware they shot the wrong person?" I asked.

DC Gallagher either ignored my comment or did not hear as he led us to bed number six. We pushed our way through the congested hallway and sidestepped other patients on gurneys along the walls. Nurses darted out briefly from behind a curtain only to disappear into another along with busy doctors. Bill unexpectedly reappeared with coffee. His presence placed a surprised look on Gallagher's face that quickly changed to an official stare.

"Lt. Popovich, what are you doing here? Aren't you supposed to be on administrative leave?" the DC questioned.

"I am. But I've been helping a friend; have a coffee Chief?" Bill stammered.

Gallagher continued down the hall and waved his arm for us to follow. When we reached an area outside the treatment room, he raised his arm with military precision, commanding us to halt. He instructed us to wait until we were asked inside. He listened briefly before slipping behind the curtain. In less than a minute, we heard people arguing on the other side of the privacy curtain.

"Where's the 'cooperation between agencies' I was promised?" a booming voice demanded.

"That's the Chief, John James," Jay informed me.

A loud but apologetic voice responded, "We didn't have anything concrete until now; we're still investigating. We'd have informed you when we had some real evidence." My local advisor identified the voice as the Special Agent in Charge of the Cleveland FBI office.

"What do you call bodies in the morgue, a by-stander shot and a wounded agent?" Chief James asked.

"Don't you think its time we worked together on this, Chief?" the SAC inquired.

"Fair enough; I want our people to cooperate and update each other on this mess," Chief James responded. The DC opened the curtain and motioned us to enter.

The SAC concluded, "From now on, this is going to be a joint investigation."

My two colleagues smiled on seeing the wounded agent was Huber. Jay and Bill did not say a word in front of their chief. Bill quickly disappeared. Amazed, I noted, "This is the agent that came to our hotel." After the SAC and Chief reconfirmed their commitment to cooperate in this investigation, they left the area.

Huber started with an apology for not telling me that he had my nephew under surveillance. He finally shared details about Jusef's involvement with Tatiana and Tarik Lazar, otherwise known as 'Lizard'. Revealing both were paid FBI informants, Bob indicated the FBI considered Lazar a small time criminal and the girl a money launderer.

"Unfortunately, Jusef is still on the loose and my other nephew is in the next bed, shot by mistake."

Bill mysteriously reappeared after *the brass* had cleared the area. His ears perked up upon hearing that Huber was about to share information on Lazar. His unit had conducted several investigations concerning Lazar's illegal operations. The detectives never directly connected him to any criminal activity nor turned any of the arrested subjects into cooperating witnesses. Huber admitted that secrecy had surrounded Lazar, but refused to acknowledge if the agency had aided him to escape prosecution. The remorseful agent detailed the events from his investigation, beginning on the day he observed Jusef with Tatiana up to the shooting.

The time had come for us to share findings of our investigation. He was surprised to learn that we had positively identified the dead male at the morgue as one of the terrorists from

Hamburg. We continued updating him on all our activities, including Gabriel's encounter with the terrorists in the coffee shop.

I concluded the fact all seven suspects are here could only mean that the headquarters of a large organization existed in Cleveland. The deduction that the terrorists were preparing to strike was unanimous. Obviously, they are planning something big, but where and when? If Huber observed Jusef on Halloween, someone else was using the Joseph Müeller credit cards in Canada to make everyone think he was still there.

We were not prepared for his personal confession. "I screwed up; I fell in love with my informant and lost my focus," Huber asserted.

"Do not condemn yourself; you are only human," I attempted to console him as we left.

On my way out, I stuck my head behind the curtain partition to look in on Gabriel. He slept peacefully unaware of the turmoil, as the staff scurried to locate an available room for him. He would be safe here. As we exited the emergency room to continue our investigation, an ER doctor was making a curbside pronouncement in the back of an ambulance.

"That's probably the girl who Huber shot. The doctor will pronounce her death before the body enters the morgue," Jay said.

We walked to the van in order to obtain a better look at this terrorist. The doctor pronounced her DOA at 0120 hours and the attendant jotted the time into his log and thanked the doctor. Jay inquired whether the victim was the one from East 105. The attendant nodded in the affirmative and opened the body bag further to afford us a better view. She was beautiful even in death, long dark hair cascading around her face. I thought if all the terrorists looked like her we did not stand a chance. At least Huber showed good taste.

The lifeless form reminded me of Nadia, my lost love in Afghanistan years ago. The only woman I actually wanted to marry was taken from me. Who could imagine a family member cut her throat for loving a foreigner? The Americans have a lot to learn about fighting an enemy that instills hatred in men's hearts.

My phone's vibration alerted me with a text message to contact my office.

"Sergeant Mayer," he answered.

"Thomas here, have you something for me?"

Mayer's last update contained the latest intelligence that revealed Acme Incorporated had links in Hamburg and Cleveland along with many other international connections. Our MEK confirmed the Lizard or *King Lizard* as his men referred to him was an actual person. This man led an elite band of fighters against the Soviets in Afghanistan. He was trained by the CIA according to rumor and a close friend to Bin Laden. Following the defeat of the Russians, the lizard disappeared and his whereabouts are unknown.

No doubt intuition, a sixth sense or years of police experience told me this lizard was in Cleveland and in charge. With no evidence to support my theory, I reflected on Jay's gut feeling about the same shooter in the three homicides. The lizard was our man. On that, I could stake my reputation.

Karl also obtained a profile on the King Lizard from an anonymous source. The profiler described him as an intelligent individual with leadership skills. According to the report, K. L. holds a major position in the terrorist hierarchy. Although he had no formal military training, he appeared to be a great military strategist. The report noted in capital letters: *HE IS NOT MUSLIM.* There was no information on religious belief, if any, or mention of family, nationality or country of birth. The profiler had narrowed K. L.'s possible nation of origin to Egypt or Saudi Arabia, a speculation based on the facts at hand.

The incomplete report fueled my theory that the Lizard was operating the Cleveland cell. The profiler had apparently constructed his report based on CIA intelligence, rumors and tribal gossip. Although the information revealed nothing as to where the man came from or any other details to provide a more accurate profile, it did contain a very important fact: The King Lizard was not Muslim, presenting an interesting question, why would a non-Muslim fight in a Jihad?

Was he in Afghanistan while I was assigned there with my unit? The tribesmen still talked about *the fighting lizards* as if only yesterday. Until now, I thought the lizards were only a legend amongst the mountain people. One tale mentioned a split among the leaders on war strategy. He is alleged to have created an army of professional fighters. Apparently, the King Lizard refused to send his men on suicide missions unless out of absolute necessity. A non-Muslim could refrain from needlessly sacrificing his men. The more I learned about this man, the less he fit the U.S. terrorist profile. He actually pretended to cooperate with the FBI, allowing him to move about freely.

Kristina and Assam's safety concerned Sonja. The usually sporadic but regular contacts had been nonexistent for several days. Karl and Sonja had the German State Department investigate the matter only to learn that they were now among the many missing in Baghdad. My fear for their wellbeing and survival was growing by the minute. Obsessed with my investigation, I had neglected to keep in touch with my family, mistakenly assuming that they were out of harms way. I made a mental note to call Sonja and request Agent Huber have his agency's office in Baghdad look into their disappearance.

"Assam, are you certain we have done the right thing?" Kristina looked from under her veil as Assam drove her Volkswagen out of the last checkpoint at the edge of the *Green Zone*. Kristina complained as she removed a silk head cover that had concealed her dark colored hair. "I feel like an informer." It did not matter; the tinted hair and scarf had done little to conceal her blue eyes. Assam's instincts told him that she must leave Iraq as soon as possible. The war had consumed the entire country at this point. The time had come to return to Germany. Each day was becoming more dangerous. She could protest all she wanted later, after they obtained permission to leave.

They needed to tell the Americans about the Mosque generating the emails. Assam suspected authorities had been aware of the Mosque and its true function for some time. He hoped their display of cooperation proved they were not insurgents or sympathizers. Maybe now, they will leave us alone.

Kristina kept an eye out for signs of danger as they drove home and away from the occupation forces. She nervously looked back toward the security zone quickly fading behind them. They traveled past an American tank plugging a gaping hole in the wall of one of Saddam's former palaces. She had not recalled earlier observing the steel monster amidst the rubble.

Assam noticed a black Mercedes with a cracked windshield in the rear view mirror. The driver shadowed the VW's every maneuver. He suspected someone was following them and made a sharp U-turn. They watched in horror as the black car swerved abruptly in a semi-circle and drew closer. I pray they are Americans.

20 | IMPENDING CATASTROPHE

Jay and Bill each looked at their watches to check the time as a matter of routine. The need to know what time something happened or where you were exactly was common in our profession. Each policeman surrenders a part of his personality one piece at a time throughout his career. Gradually, they act similarly except for minor individual traits. I followed suit, noting the time and date: One-thirty in the morning, November 11.

"Today is 11-11. This is not good," I declared, sensing an impending catastrophe.

"Why?"

"The 11th of September, the 11th of March, the 11th of July and now the 11th of November—they are going to strike today: the eleventh day of the eleventh month. I believe whatever they came to do is already started," I proclaimed. My revelation was followed by dead silence.

Bill quipped, "It's obvious to the most casual observer and evident to a well-trained mind that the wheels are in motion."

On the other side of town, radio traffic was beginning to pick up as more emergency vehicles were dispatched to the Flats Area. The field commander authorized the radio communication center to ignore district boundaries. The top brass now started to make their presence known.

SIU Superintendent Steve Taylor contacted Jay on his mobile phone. Bill knew that they were in for something either very good or very bad by the expression on his friend's face. Bill informed me that the call probably signaled another homicide or a bombing because of the hour and the caller. I acknowledged Bill with a nod. Jay grinned and confirmed Bill's assessment. As Jay took in the details, he grimaced at the assignment and exclaimed, "They blew up some bridges and a ship in the Flats."

We all shared the apprehension that Jusef and Ali might be involved. Is this the beginning of a larger attack or was it finished? I dreaded the thought of another turf battle between the federal agents and locals. Then I realized that no one else was coming to assist. Cleveland's safety forces were the only defenders available at this hour.

Once again, Jay attached the blue strobe light to the roof and we sped away with flashing light and siren. A feeling of trepidation came over me about Jusef, hoping that my worst fear had not come true. Not knowing what bridges were out, Jay took the most direct route. As we rounded the East Bank on Old River Road, the destruction astonished us. A Railroad Bridge was twisted and torn, pieces of steel track hung motionless over the river ready to snap at any moment. Metal bits and pieces had been blown off the trestle and strewn along the two riverbanks.

Jay stopped the car in order to take in the panoramic of devastation. Three bridges lay on the valley floor or the river bottom. The banks beneath the railroad bridge resembled a scrap yard. The lift and swing bridge skeletons hovered over the black water. Dead pieces of metal continued to plummet from the dying structures. The crippled ore boat drifted aimlessly in the water without her control tower. Rescuers searched for bodies of the missing crew in the icy river. Anyone lucky enough to survive the collision would have surely perished from hypothermia. God, wake me from this nightmare! Where was homeland security—how did they allow terrorists to penetrate America's heartland?

Unfortunately, all three veterans knew the attack was real and that they must capture those responsible. Senseless killings and utter annihilation that accompanied wars, revolutions, insurgencies and religious strife were all too familiar to the trio. War was considered legalized murder, an exclusive right of the state, no matter the reason.

Regretfully, I informed my colleagues, "This is the work of Al-Qaeda, or the Taliban, professionally orchestrated and quite similar to attacks I remembered in Afghanistan."

A buzz came from my phone. At this hour, the message could only mean bad news that usually came in threes. Father's shaky voice notified me Kristina was dead, killed in an explosion along with Assam. He reported that on the way back to her apartment, a suicide bomber stopped in a car alongside theirs and detonated a bomb, killing them and their attacker. Hearing this news again left me numb and speechless. First, Gabriel, then the bombing and now Kristina—what more can happen?

Wolfgang fought back his sobbing voice, "This is difficult to take. You are not supposed to bury your children. Oh, God, there may not be anything left to bury—" he wept.

Somehow, I mustered up the courage to console my father, reminding him of the people he had helped through psychological illnesses and personal problems. How fortunate mother and Sonja were to have him there in their time of need. I sensed father's helplessness from the voice on the other side of the ocean.

"Thank you. I feel better now that I was able to speak with you. How are you and Gabriel doing?"

"Maybe you had better sit down." I said and started into the story, reassuring him that Gabriel was all right, but injured and in the hospital. I related the facts without going into pertinent details.

"Thank God. When are you coming home?"

"Soon, but not immediately; I cannot leave Gabriel and we have found where Jusef has been, but not him specifically. There was a terrorist attack here and I am assisting the Cleveland Police. I have a favor to ask. Would you please notify Sonja about Gabriel's injury, stressing he is all right and expected to be released from hospital tomorrow?"

"Yes, I will. Thomas, I understand you may not be able to tell me what you are doing, but I know you will do the right thing. Be careful. I love you; may God watch over you."

"My phone is signaling another call that I must take. Tell the others I love them as well. Goodbye for now."

Mayer had obtained the facts surrounding Kristina and Assam's deaths. Although far away, his voice was comforting, though I detected a note of surprise when he learned the news of their deaths had already reached me. The officials suspect a car loaded with 500 pounds of military grade explosives blew up next to them, spraying the entire area with shrapnel from a 30mm shell. People were peppered with bits of hot shredded metal 30 meters from the blast center; several cars were also set ablaze when their gas tanks exploded, flinging them through the air. The bomber stopped alongside them at a traffic light and detonated his explosive device. Investigators believe the assassin followed them from the green zone after they reported a mosque that was recruiting terrorists. On their way home, Kristina and Assam stopped at an intersection, where the suicide bomber killed them. Sadly, the authorities said they were aware of the mosque and believed the bomber was following them in the days prior to the blast.

I pressed him for information on the identities of the victims, clinging to the notion there could have been a mistake made on the ID's. His words and thoroughness dashed my false hope. The investigators in Iraq traced their identities through DNA tests and the ownership of the bombed vehicle through the confidential vehicle identification number.

"Who determined they were at the mosque?" I asked.

"Security logs showed their arrival and departure times in the visitor's roster. They suspect someone on the inside passed the information to the insurgents. The tragedy is that this mosque was already on a terrorist watch list. Is there anything further you would like me to do?"

"Please look in on my family and assist them with their needs. I hope to return in a few days. Now, let me inform you of what has happened here so far." Mayer was updated on our activities in Cleveland. A beep on my mobile signaled an incoming call.

"My phone has another call. Later."

"Good luck, Thomas."

Seeing my sister's number, I switched to her call.

"Thomas, what have you done to my son? You promised me he would be safe with you," a familiar voice shrieked.

"Calm down. He is safe. There was an unfortunate incident, and he sustained a minor wound to his leg."

Sonja questioned, "How in the hell did he get shot? Where were you?"

"We were looking for Jusef and a shooting occurred between the FBI and several suspects."

"Oh, so that just *happened*?"

"Yes, this evening we were close to rescuing Jusef when all hell broke loose unexpectedly. Gabriel located Jusef and we were on our way to bring him back. These are the only details we have at the present time."

"Do not tell me that police crap. I want to know why Gabriel was shot."

"You can call him at University Hospital. He is in a room for observation and he should be released by tomorrow. Believe me—I am sorry for what happened. If I could change any of this, I would. I will give you the phone number."

"Okay. Thomas, are you all right?"

"I am heartbroken at the loss of our Kristina and your Assam. Their deaths have yet to register in my mind."

"This is the same for me. I keep waiting for an email or phone call; I cannot believe they are both gone," she cried.

"I am so very sorry. I will be coming home soon to help you with any arrangements."

"Do not say that. That was the last thing Assam said before he left for Baghdad. Thomas, be careful. I love you. Bring my Gabriel home to me, please," she continued sobbing.

"I will as soon as he can travel."

"Promise me."

"Promise; I love you, too. We must not tell Gabriel about their deaths until we are safe at home with family," I suggested.

"Whatever you think is best. Goodbye."

As the deadly trio left the store on E 105, they looked up at the circling helicopter; its overhead presence startled Jusef as he crouched in an attempt to avoid detection. He wondered aloud. "Are they looking for us? Do they know we are here?" His two comrades were pleased with his instant reaction to the perceived threat.

"It is possible, but highly improbable that they are looking for us," Lazar coolly remarked, knowing Jusef's airborne menace was only a news helicopter. Besides, he was confident that no one knew anything about the plot to strike, and by tomorrow it would be too late. He added, "The police helicopters have been out of service for two years."

"Why would they eliminate a valuable component of their security force during a war?" Jusef posed.

"It does not matter—all the better for us!"

Yassar related to the young warriors apprehension to the menace in the clouds. He remembered becoming alarmed at the sound of rotating blades and aircraft engines—let alone the crafts deadly presence. Helicopters used to scare him too. In time, Jusef will grow out of the Middle East mindset and assimilate his new surroundings. He will also learn that not all flying objects are enemy aircraft.

The three men entered the silver SUV. Yassar drove to the warehouse, parking the vehicle along side the neglected black metal structure. Jusef's entire body tingled with excitement; the day of the impending attack had come, with the Lizard in charge and issuing commands to field units from one of a half-dozen cell phones clipped to his belt. They walked inside the empty building except for one guard concealed in the shadows behind a van. A black Hum-V and a white van were barely visible in the dimly lighted warehouse.

Omar stepped out from behind the van and joined them, saying, "Mick is sleeping in the Hum-V."

Lazar led them into the front office and displayed aerial photos of power plants, electrical grids and bridges. Handing maps to Yassar and Jusef, Lazar informed them, "These are your assignments. Most of the charges have been previously set to go off."

He handed them both a backpack, each containing several cell phones numbered according to corresponding targets, and instructed, "You may have to attach explosives to two or three towers we could not get to. Everything you need is in your assigned vehicle. Are there any questions?"

Impressed with the maps, Jusef asked, "How did you obtain these maps?"

Lazar answered, "The Internet is a great source of information," pointing to the map, "remember, the ones marked in red have been armed; you still must arm the blue ones. Is there anything else?" No one responded. "Excellent, after the attack, everyone will go directly to their new locations as planned. Under no circumstances are you to return to any of the places here."

Following Lizards briefing, on cue as if a secret signal had been sent, Yassar and Omar went to work tearing down the map area. Omar poured petrol on the plywood frames while his partner continued to stack paperwork on the woodpile. The noise woke up Mick in the passenger seat. Jusef did not recognize him without the Halloween mask. Lazar handed Jusef a 9mm pistol with several extra clips, a map and a brown vinyl shaving kit. "Here is something for the bartender."

Jusef drove out of the warehouse with the lights off, pistol tucked under his belt and several loaded magazines in his pocket. Mick excitedly opened the kit. Several blocks away, Jusef could see orange flames shooting into the sky in his rear view mirror.

21 | DARK AGES

WE WALKED TOWARD DEPUTY CHIEF GALLAGHER THROUGH splashes of red and blue snowflakes. An eerie scene was created from flashing strobe lights on rows of emergency vehicles. Bill pointed at a group of policemen, "DC Gallagher is already here setting up a command post."

The DC said, "Glad to see you guys. All hell is breaking loose."

Bill inquired, "Where at?"

"—the whole damned city and the entire country: New York, Washington, Chicago...all the big cities are under attack. We set up a command post at city hall and we're operating on emergency power. The Mayor has contacted the governor, requesting National Guard Troops. We were informed that there is no one to send because most of our guard is in Iraq. All remaining guard units in Ohio are being activated and setting up command centers for rescue and recovery operations in areas where power is still available. Apparently, we're on our own." He paused, checking our facial expressions for any reaction.

"This reminds me of the Tet Offensive when the VC attacked every major city in South Vietnam," Bill stated.

I stressed, "Is this the beginning or the end? These attackers were not sent on a suicide mission. They are just getting started."

"So far, we have two dead suicide bombers over at the Columbus Road Bridge," Gallagher said.

"I have photos of the seven terrorists from my city, including the one that we identified at the morgue. I would like to see if any of my photos match the bridge bombers."

Gallagher continued, "Do you want to hear the real kicker?"

"What's that, Chief?" Bill inquired as his phone rang, "Excuse me, Chief."

"Lieutenant, we checked that out for you. The store was completely empty; no signs of life; locked up tighter than a drum," Bill's detective reported.

"Thanks. I'm at the river command post if you need anything. I think they're going to have everyone go back into uniform for the next couple of days."

The narcotics detective started, "Sir, I—I."

"I know; your hair and the beard; there will probably be some exceptions."

"Thanks, LT."

Bill hung up.

DC Gallagher looked at Bill from under furrowed eyebrows, "Lieutenant, still just helping a friend with a missing relative?"

The DC went on, "If you guys don't mind, I'd like to continue what I was saying. The national head of Homeland Security called our governor and ordered him to send Ohio guardsmen to assist federal troops in Washington, DC. When the governor informed Homeland Security, there were no guardsmen to send, so the Homeland Security Chief immediately asked if we had any additional police officers to spare. I can only imagine what was said, but we'll never know who hung up on whom first."

Puzzled, I added, "This lack of coordination and division during a national crisis is unbelievable."

"We've lost control of our own safety to federal bureaucrats who seized power and took charge in the name of homeland security," Bill complained.

"I never realized how divided your country is; how can you win this war under these conditions?"

"This won't be easy, but we'll persevere and win. We're Americans."

DC Gallagher assumed command, walking among his officers, checking on his supervisors needs and conversing with his troops.

I agreed with Bill, "You may be correct in comparing this attack to the Tet Offensive; except these saboteurs are not here to capture your cities; they have come to cripple them by attacking your infrastructure."

A mobile Cleveland Police command center vehicle drove into the parking area where the rescue vehicles were scattered. We followed DC Gallagher to the command post like homing pigeons. A uniformed officer opened the door and we entered the converted mobile home, equipped with a cramped kitchen area, lavatory and a command center at the rear of the vehicle. A dozen radios chattered on separate frequencies while six outside telephones were positioned on a two-foot railing along the sides of the console. Eight 9-inch TV monitors displayed activities outside from several viewpoints and angles.

Looking at the monitors, I commented, "No one could sneak up on us with all this. The TV cameras cover every angle."

Bill laughed. "This RV used to belong to a drug dealer who frequently traveled to Florida to pick up his dope. We confiscated the vehicle from him." Pointing to the monitors, he continued, "He didn't want to get ripped off by his competitors or nabbed by the police. Actually, he was quite paranoid."

The Command Post door opened and Chief James walked in.

"I thought I'd come over and see how everything is going," he said. "Truthfully, I had to get out of city hall; there were too many politicians getting in the way."

DC Gallagher asked, "Any more updates on the attacks?"

"They attacked three major cities in Ohio and information is trickling in on possibly dozens attacked nationwide."

"Chief, do we know how many casualties?" DC asked.

"Surprisingly, there is very little loss of life; the infrastructure appears to be the target of this attack. We do know the power grid is out from New York to Toledo."

"That includes us," DC said.

"This is going to be worse than the black out of '02. They damaged not mere substations; a whole series of transmission towers were knocked down, disrupting the power supply," Jay exclaimed.

"Not only that, they blew up major spans of interstate highway and railroad bridges. There is not one interstate route completely intact," the chief said.

"How much of our telecommunication system have been destroyed?" DC inquired.

"All communications have been affected. We're operating on emergency generators and cell phones," he replied. "We are fortunate most of our police officers have cell phones. We have been able to mobilize our 'off-duties' and other safety personnel. I have instructed patrol units to check all major bridge spans and stop traffic until the bridges are inspected—the ones that are still standing. I've ordered all working utility personnel to be checked out to see if they are legitimate. DC Collins is working on the deployment of officers as they report for duty and vehicle assignments," the chief outlined. "By the way, who is making the coffee here? We are fortunate that the command post has a generator and propane tanks. I'll expect a cup waiting for me when I return from the head."

"Hey Chief—," an officer called out from the rear communications center, "Detroit was not affected. They have full power and they went on full alert and activated their safety forces."

"What do you think of that? In my mind, that leaves little doubt as to who is behind this mess," the chief speculated.

I added, "I think we can safely assume that we know where to concentrate our next search. Before we do anything, may I suggest radiation testing at the bomb sites?"

Jay responded, "We have to contact the feds—my unit is not equipped to measure radiation levels."

"Sergeant Andrewski, you have a call on line two," the communications officer called out.

Jay took the call and reported, "Chief, my unit has just completed a ballistics test on the pellets recovered from the homicide victim's burned body. The pellets were a perfect match to the sample from the 9mm pistol belonging to the suspect that Lt. Popovich shot."

I commented, "This confirms our suspicions regarding the terrorists' involvement in the store owners' murders.

A truck wore attached magnetic signs for the Ajax Electrical Contractor Company. The white panel utility van rolled up to the underground vault on East Ninth and Euclid Avenue in the downtown business center. The yellow caution lights and emergency flashers from the truck were the only signs of light. Two workers wearing white hard hats and orange vests got out, placed orange construction cones around the street vault behind the truck, and lifted the cover with a long pry bar. Yassar descended into the manhole while Omar stood lookout.

His mangled fingers opened a large canvas bag and began removing sticks of C4. He methodically went to work strapping the explosives to the underground fiber optic, electrical cable and other utilities in conduit that fed and connected the financial and commercial nerve center to the world. Shining his light down the labyrinth of dark damp tunnels carrying miles of cables, Yassar removed his rubber gloves to more quickly wire the center of the template where everything met.

Around 0230, a spotlight from a patrol temporarily blinded Omar's vision, silently announcing the police presence. He began squinting at the black and white car fifty feet away and crawling in his direction. Inching a 9mm pistol from his coat pocket, he

drew and fired at the officers in the car. They immediately bailed
out and rapidly returned fire from a prone position.

"Three Twenty-Two…—East 9th and Euclid—we're being
shot at—" one of the officers screamed into the microphone.

Muzzle flashes pierced the black streets, accompanied by the
cracking sounds of a battle that echoed through the urban canyon.
Bullets whizzed back and forth until Omar went down.

"Hey, are you alright?" the driver called out to his partner on
the other side of the car.

"Yeah, how about you?" he responded.

"I didn't get hit, but I banged my knee when I hit he ground;
hurts like hell."

Upon hearing the gunshots from above, Yassar quickly removed four white phosphorus grenades from his bag. Pulling the
pins, he threw two in each direction of the tunnel. With seconds
to spare, he dialed the cell phone attached to the C4.

An orange eruption came from the vault, shaking the street
and shattering windows on the closest buildings, followed by four
minor underground explosions. The C4 erupted through the
street plummeting the phosphorus in a fireworks display before it
gravitated to earth in a plume of heavy gray smoke.

"We'd better call this one in—we're going to need some help,"
one officer yelled as they scrambled for cover.

Back at the command center, Jay, Bill and I viewed the destruction from the post televisions. TV station helicopters by now were
surveying the aftermath from early dawn light, aided by reflec-
tions off the snow-covered landscape. The best way to describe
the assaults on the Inner Belt bridges and cross-town overpasses
is to say they cut the city in half. A few sections defied gravity,
resembling small parking lots a hundred-fifty feet in the sky where
earlier the twelve-lane highway over Valley View was blown up.
Police and service employees were at work barricading the edge

of the cliffs above. Some roads below were already blocked by fallen concrete. Any remaining debris from shattered foundations had their tops ripped apart, exposing bent protruding rebar with a look of windswept hair. The parts that still stood on the remaining legs were capable of collapsing any second. We stood watching the astonishing pictures.

"Look, there!" I pointed.

All eyes focused on one of the monitor screens. We followed Jay outside the post to get a better view. We watched in horror as a pair of headlights from atop the inner belt bridge approached the missing span. The two white dots plunged into the darkness as they went over the edge. Hundreds of feet below, we stood helplessly viewing, unable to stop the inevitable catastrophe.

The anticipated muffled crunch was heard in the distance.

Bill shouted, "There's another car."

Another pair of white dots traveled toward the missing span and impending demise in the valley below.

He called out from the nearest police car radio, "This is 8200. Get some marked cars at both ends of the Cuyahoga River inner belt bridge spans."

An officer near him remarked, "Lieutenant, did you see those cars go off the bridge?"

Bill called out, "Yeah—get your ass up there. Now!"

Radio returned, "We have no cars at present. We'll put it on the list."

Bill immediately conscripted two police officers from the command area.

"You, take this car and here, you take that one and stop those cars going over the edge!" he pointed.

Bill followed us back inside the command post.

I handed a cup of coffee to him and commented, "Well done, LT."

Looking over at Jay thumbing through his wallet, Bill asked, "What are you doing, paying for the coffee?"

Displaying his open billfold, he remarked, "None of these credit cards are any good without electricity. I only have twenty-seven dollars cash on hand."

"If you need some money, I still have a few travelers' checks," I offered.

Jay came up with, "Refrigeration and freezers have stopped; fresh food will soon be in short supply. How much walleye can one eat in the next 24 hours? I've got a freezer full."

Bill gave a gloomier prediction, "We must prepare for riots and looting that inevitably follow this type of disaster."

I sadly remarked, "Your city has just been turned into a war zone."

Jay suggested, "At the moment, there is nothing further you can do here. Would you like a car to return you to the hospital to check up on your nephew?"

An unfamiliar number appeared as my phone vibrated, interrupting Jay's question. A welcome voice pleasantly greeted, "Hello, Thomas?"

"Mary, are you and your son okay?"

"Yes, don't worry about us. You have been on my mind ever since you returned. I really never expected to see you again."

"I understand. Where are you?"

"I'm assigned with another officer to protect some cell phone towers in the metro parks, but that isn't why I called. With all that is going on, I wanted you to know before you left that I love you."

Without thinking, I whispered into the phone, "I think I love you, too."

"What? Did you say something?"

I blurted out, "I love you, Mary!" There was a brief pause following my revelation.

She continued, "There is something that I have to tell you…" —Silence.

"Mary, are you still there? Mary?"

The signal was cut off, ending our conversation.

A man in an SUV activated his mobile phone from several hundred meters away, causing the cell phone tower to blow up. Both wounded officers lay motionless several meters from their position. Following the explosion, the SUV driver continued on his way.

Jay contacted me at University Hospital, while I was collecting Gabriel, following his release. He phoned an update on Mary's condition from Lutheran Hospital across town. My love lay unconscious from the explosion at the towers she was guarding. Apparently, the explosive charges had been previously planted and activated from a synchronized cell phone number.

I struggled to refocus control of my emotions and carry on in a professional manner. Unfortunately, each disturbing call concerning people I cared for thrust another dagger into my heart. Jay's arrangements for us to return home could not have come at a worse time.

Our driver informed us Toronto was the closest functioning airport. Detroit had been placed under military control. We drove to Lutheran Hospital, contrary to Jay's advice, knowing I had to see her.

Nothing prepared me for Mary's helpless condition, machines and tubes connected to her arms and face, displaying her struggle to survive. I leaned over, caressed her hair, and kissed my Irish Rebel on the cheek. It did not matter if she knew, but it was important to me.

22 | ESCAPE AND EVASION

As the jumbo airplane pierced through the cloud cover and leveled off, the Lufthansa pilot announced, "For our flight from Toronto International Airport to Hamburg, Germany, we are projecting fair weather and a smooth flight for most of the trip. I hope you will sit back and enjoy the flight."

"What about finding Jusef?" Gabriel asked.

"Once things are settled back home I must return to America. I will send for you later. Right now, your mother needs you."

Gabriel studied my face a minute, and then posed, "You are exceptionally quiet; I sense there is something you are not telling me."

My mind was preoccupied with the search for the correct words to tell him his father had been assassinated. The telling without invoking hate or revenge would take some doing. I did not realize I was projecting cracks in my normally stone-faced expression. The only solution was to make an official announcement, "I must share some bad news with you."

"Is Jusef dead?" he speculated.

"I honestly do not know if he is dead or alive or his whereabouts."

His young worried face tensed up in anticipation of the blow I was about to deliver. I slipped into my police personality as I fought back my tears. Any more delay would only make things worse.

"Your father and Kristina were killed in an explosion."

"How—where?"

"In Baghdad, a suicide bomber blew up their car."

"This cannot be true."

"I am sorry to have to tell you."

"The Americans are at fault with their illegal occupation."

"How can you blame the Americans?"

"They forced him to remain in Iraq and search for WMDs that did not exist." He looked directly at me, "Even you said the WMDs were a lie to justify going to war."

"Yes, I understand, but there were other reasons."

"Do not defend them. They killed my father with their phony war!" Gabriel folded his arms, body trembling and looked away.

Upon hearing my own words, I was speechless. One of my deepest fears was taking hold of me. Gabriel was beginning to sound like Jusef. Right then, I made a solemn promise to continue my quest to stop Jusef once Gabriel was home and safe.

Who are these people that divide families and turn men into killers? All good people must band together to fight this evil from spreading throughout the world. I feared for the future, recalling Winston Churchill's prediction: *The wars of the people will be more terrible than those of the kings.*

Halfway to Toledo, the black Mercedes was ready to leave the rendezvous point. Lazar's one luxury was the most expensive model carried by Mercedes-Benz, equipped with every option: armored body, bulletproof windows and tires, complete with survival kit in a fireproof interior including the trunk. A Middle East Monarch sent the car over during a medical visit to the Cleveland Clinic. The vehicle was later donated for Lazar's use and kept in his warehouse along with other supplies to be used in the attack. He could never leave such a beautiful piece of machinery for the enemy. His associates rumored the car cost a half million euros.

While Lazar surveyed the dark empty rest area parking lot, the wipers shoved snow off in a mechanical rhythm. Once certain the rest stop was deserted, he drove to the vending area for coffee and left the car idling, radio spewing out emergency government broadcasts. The evil genius went to check out the unlit machines, deposited the exact change and waited for coffee. To his surprise, the coins rolled straight to the return. Trying again, the same deposit gave the same result. Now I see: the machines are dark; the restrooms; the parking lot; everything is dark. Reality had set in. The electricity was out because there was no power. Success!

Jusef carefully drove back onto the snow-covered road toward I-90 West, taking precautions not to be caught. Inclined to push the Hum-V accelerator to the floor and fly away to the rendezvous point, he held back the impulse and maintained the speed limit. There was no sense being caught after everything had gone smoothly thus far. Patience, he thought. The stiff, silent passenger next to him was beginning to show signs of rigidity. An elastic rubber band similar to ones used by emergency medical technicians tying off wounds remained above the man's elbow. The dashboard lights illuminated an open zippered cloth pouch with a kit for using drugs.

Headlights reflecting off the wall caused Lazar to look at a passing car. Jusef was driving toward the restroom building. He quickly abandoned the vehicle after seeing no one around except for a lone black Mercedes.

The black car drove past the Hum-V. From the Mercedes lowered window, the driver called out, "Jusef, get in. Ahura Mazda be praised," Lazar prayed for thanksgiving.

"Mick is dead. I think he overdosed."

Shrugging his shoulder, he replied, "Truth is, he was an addict who received a *hot shot.*"

"Is that a new type of bullet?"

"No. A *hot shot* is a high dose of narcotic that causes a quick painless death to the victim, with or without their cooperation. They usually administer the drug to themselves, but in rare cases they require assistance. The police will presume he is merely the victim of another overdose."

Jusef smiled, "I am pleased to see you."

"I am pleased as well."

"Your expensive suit and tie compliment your car. You appear to be a successful businessman."

"Yes, my attire and vehicle will serve our purpose in Detroit. How did your mission go?" Lazar took note of the leather gloves on his protégé. "Did you keep the gloves on?"

Removing his gloves, Jusef spoke, "Yes, sir, as instructed. I toppled the electrical towers in Cleveland with ease. I became more proficient with each one. There were no guards or anyone to witness my activities in the isolated woods. The only hindrances were the terrain and the weather. The Hum-V helped overcome the conditions. Before starting the vehicle, I gave Mike the kit as you asked. Immediately, he tore open the bag, prepared an injection and plunged the needle into his arm. When he passed out, I stopped to check him for a pulse—he was dead." *How could anyone die so quickly without actually being shot?* Jusef left him with the hypodermic syringe still dangling from his arm by the needle. Mick lay slumped in the passenger seat with his head against the door as if asleep.

"Continue—"

"The C4, cell phone detonators and duct tape all worked well. My training in Hamburg with Ali taught us that the charges could easily blow the metal legs and cripple the towers. Unbelievably, the entire structure crashed to the ground so quickly, I saw the explosion before I heard the blasts. When the cables hit the ground, they arced and hissed like giant electrical snakes. I was amazed that I was not injured. Everything was so simple. I strapped the charges to the metal legs with this amazing tape. There were only a few towers that I had to arm." He reached in his coat pocket, pulled out and displayed a half roll of duct tape.

"Is that all?"

"As planned, we eliminated two and three sets of towers every three kilometers, continuing along the path for 30 kilometers. My mission ended too soon. I could have done more."

Caught up in the excitement of the attack, Jusef had temporarily forgotten Tatiana. Winning was exhilarating. A jolt of adrenaline rushed through every nerve in his body. He wondered was it always like this following an attack, as he savored the moment.

Lazar congratulated, "You have helped send a message across America, while our enemies sleep. You have done well."

Lazar searched for anything on the radio and found a single station broadcasting news: "*If you're just getting up, and you can hear this, stay home. Most of your cities are not safe out there. The entire country is under attack! Speaking with our field correspondent in Cleveland, Ohio, Robert Flagg, what are experiencing there? Can you give us an update? Jim, we are broadcasting live from the heart of the city. Everything is blacked out except for emergency lighting. Reports continue to trickle in. We do know that some main power transmission lines have been blown up across Ohio and there are outages from New York to Chicago. We are also receiving reports of entire regions of the country in complete darkness. Here in Cleveland as in other parts of the United States, interstates and railroad bridges have been destroyed, cutting vehicle transportation. The lack of traffic signals coupled with the weather has caused numerous accidents and travel is impossible in most cities. Some locations have no running water, streetlights, computers, and TV or radio communications. Cell phones are becoming the only means of communication and even they are jamming up. Authorities are attempting to set up command centers to maintain order and coordinate rescue and repair operations in each state. Gas stations are unable to pump fuel without power. The police are asking everyone to remain inside. Back to you, Jim—thank you, Robert Flagg reporting live on the scene in Cleveland.*

From the state capital, we have additional information. The governor was asked for comment. He responded, "The attack appears to be well coordinated, swift and almost invisible. Here in Ohio, attackers have turned our major cities back to the dark ages. We favored oil as a primary source of energy and took electrical power for granted. Without electricity, millions of gallons of gasoline may as well have stayed in the ground."

"We'll have further updates as they become available, as long as we can stay on the air. This just in: The President has declared a national emergency and requests that people remain calm. American Forces around the world are on high alert. From New York to Los Angeles, rescuers on

the graveyard shift are the only witnesses to the magnitude of the destruction. The attack so far appears to be directed at the major cities of the United States. No country or groups have taken responsibility. Several governors have declared a state of emergency, including Ohio. All safety forces and medical personnel are asked to report to duty. Members of the National Guard are asked to report to their respective units or to local law enforcement. All schools and businesses are closed due to lack of power. More news will follow as we receive it. Keep tuned in for any breaking news."

He turned down the volume to speak, "This will be an interesting turn of events. Now they will experience the living conditions they impose on our people. Let us see how they cope with war."

The news reporter continued, *"In homes across the nation, people are beginning to wake up. No heat, no lights, no coffee, no TV, no computers and no ATMs.*

Another field operation was checking in with a buzz on Lazar's blackberry.

He asked Jusef, "Can you please read what you see on the screen?"

"I can read some of the words. Plant 6 closed," he slowly enunciated.

"Very good, go on."

"Acme, Inc. job site 3 and Acme Inc. Field Office 10 closed… storm damage?" he asked in Arabic.

"Please continue in English," he said. With each announcement, Lazar smiled at the news.

"Coyote Enterprises Manufacturing Center will need supplies for project X at new job site. Where are Tatiana and Ali? Are they safe? Are they okay?" Jusef asked.

"They are on another assignment. Have plants 7, 9 or 11 checked in? How about numbers 13 and 16?" Lazar questioned.

"No other reports from what I see."

"We were fortunate. I hope the others did as well as we did. I only lost four out of twenty cells."

Jusef stared in the side mirror at the emerging thin red line that signaled the dawn. The road sign read *Toledo 60 Miles, Detroit 135 Miles*. With that, the young warrior had dozed off. Lazar picked up the blackberry and scrolled the messages looking for signs of Yassar and Omar (#7), Tatiana (#13) and any other cells that had not reported. No new messages; a tear swelled in his eye. *I must learn to keep my promise and never again become attached to anyone.*

Waking just outside Detroit to the sound of Johnny Cash singing *Ring of Fire*, Jusef asked, "Are the radio stations back in service?"

"No, this is a CD. I like listening to country music. The songs are about life. The radio is broadcasting emergency updates on our successful attacks. We took out the power grids in Ohio, Pennsylvania, New York and many other places according to news reports."

"I feel like I have done something of benefit to my brothers."

"You have done a good job. Now you are a true soldier. There were others across the country, all striking at the same moment. We launched a thousand stones at the United States and you were but one of them. We have achieved a great victory for our side."

"I am proud to serve as a soldier fighting for our people against the western democracies that are destroying our culture and stealing our oil. I wish to continue our fight for Allah like you."

"What do you mean, Allah? I am not a Muslim; I am Zoroastrian."

"Then why do you fight?"

"I fight for goodness in the world and the right to be left alone. I hope our message will awaken the American people to what their government is doing secretly in their name so they put an end to the lies and occupation of our lands. Then we can live in peace and harmony as Ahura Mazda intended for all his creations."

Hearing the Lizard's words, Jusef's thoughts returned to Tatiana—peace, harmony and love—especially love. *I will make my own peace with her. Let the others fight.*

Lizard turned up his recording of Johnny Horton's Battle of New Orleans: ...*they ran through the briars and they ran through the brambles where a rabbit wouldn't go...we beat the mighty British in the Gulf of Mexico.*

EPILOGUE

THE ACTIONS OF ONE INDIVIDUAL DO NOT BRING DOWN AN ENTIRE civilization, society or government because humans are not pure in their causes. We are neither completely Spartan Warrior nor Evil Demon. Terrorists are personally responsible for their deeds. We all act in ways that change our destinies each day a little at a time.

Conversely, the actions of a civilization, society or government can bring us down if we allow them to, each day, a little at a time. How many seeds of hatred have been planted around the world or how many more stones are left? We may never know. However, there will always be those who will fight for their beliefs if only with stones.

No two men are alike, and both of them are happy for it.

—*Morris Mandel*

ENDNOTES

Page 127 Kahlil Gibran paraphrase from *The Listener* by Kahlil Gibran

Page 200 Winston Churchill quote from *Power Quotes* by Daniel B. Baker

ALSO CHECK OUT JOHN AND PHIL'S OTHER WORKS COMING SOON:

NO COMMON SENSE compares modern tyranny with the colonists under King George by retracing American history. Thomas Paine ended his pamphlets to his fellow Americans with the anonymous name *Common Sense*, but how would he address our government today?

BUSH WARS follows German Investigator Thomas Freiderich's quest to seek his nephew turned terrorist as re-emergent cells prepare to launch a new wave of attacks on America.

MILLSTONE MURDERS begins as a boater spots a body drifting in Lake Erie. Cleveland Police discover several more bound corpses floating with their index fingers and thumbs missing. A detective learns the victims are all priests. Who would kill a priest and why?